The Kingdom Queen

The Kingdom Queen

A Medieval Novella

J. T. Page Jr.

iUniverse

THE KINGDOM QUEEN
A Medieval Novella

iUniverse books may be ordered through booksellers or by contacting:

iUniverse
1663 Liberty Drive
Bloomington, IN 47403
www.iuniverse.com
1-800-Authors (1-800-288-4677)

ISBN: 978-1-5320-2956-1 (sc)
ISBN: 978-1-5320-2955-4 (e)

Library of Congress Control Number: 2017915487

Print information available on the last page.

iUniverse rev. date: 10/31/2017

To Gretchen, my forever sweetheart.

Chivalry: It's the little boy that kisses my hand, the young man who holds the door open for me, and the old man who tips his hat to me. None of it is a reflection of me, but a reflection of them.
—Donna Lynn Hope

The motto of chivalry is also the motto of wisdom; to serve all, but to love only one.
—Honoré de Balzac

The greatest thing you'll ever learn is just to love and be loved in return.
—Eden Ahbez

PROLOGUE

THE KINGDOM AD 1110 THE HIGH MIDDLE AGES

Theo sighed and smiled as he looked out toward the lake while the other children played. He was as happy as he could ever recall. And despite his young age, Theo appreciated such things as the morning calm.

He turned his gaze and focused on the royal tent. The nearby announcement bell recently painted red caught his eye. One of the king's guards walked his post. The large tent was pitched alongside the lake that was nearly surrounded by a thick, black forest. The calm, glistening body of water was just a few minutes' walk below the magnificent kingdom castle.

Theo took a few steps closer to the water and thanks to the flawless weather noted that the castle was perfectly mirrored on the lake's surface. He turned back and saw young Princess Margarethe and her best friend, Lady Marianne, playing with the other children. A few ladies from the court watched over them.

Theo looked again in the direction of the tent and saw Queen Annemarie seated in the middle of the wide entrance, smiling sweetly at the children, and nodding in agreement as Lady Lorraine, Theo's mother, spoke to her. Theo imagined they were speaking of his father, Sir Josef, who had been knighted by King Johann in a great ceremony the day prior.

At the far edge of the lake, a Saracen marauder stealthily took aim with a crossbow and silently eliminated one of the king's guards. Seconds later, only young Theo noticed when an arrow struck a second guard, the one standing near the announcement bell. The guard awkwardly fell backward near the royal tent. Theo shouted warnings to the princess and her playmates and ran toward the royal tent, but Queen Annemarie and Lady Lorraine were engrossed in pleasant conversation and were unaware of the attack.

"Run to the castle! Run!" yelled Theo as he raced to the bell near the queen's tent. He saw Queen Annemarie leap to her feet while Lady Lorraine looked shocked and almost frozen in place. Theo noted several marauders in the distance closing in on the lake from the far edge of the forest. He reached the bell and began pounding it furiously with the attached mallet. Theo saw two other guards appear from behind the royal tent, race toward the attackers, and take up positions near the bell.

"Lead everyone to the castle! Now!" Theo shouted to the queen and his mother.

A fierce-looking Saracen stepped out from behind a nearby tree and ran toward the clanging bell. He stopped and took careful aim with his crossbow. He would silence the bell by silencing the boy.

1

Innsbruck, Austria
Present Day

The cab pulled to a stop in the Old City area of Innsbruck. Cubby exited first. He was followed by his older sister, Carmen, while their mother, Friederun, paid the driver.

Cubby put his hands on his hips, looked up, and surveyed the imposing church in front of him with his bright-blue eyes. Known locally as the Hofkirche, the sixteenth-century structure contained a treasure trove of art and lore. It was the final resting place for many, including one of Austria's great heroes, Andreas Hofer, who had lived two hundred years earlier. But that's a story for another day.

"Is Otto going to be our guide again today?" asked Cubby as his mother climbed from the cab.

Friederun smiled. "Yes, and I think we are really fortunate to have had someone like him show us around Innsbruck this past week. Your father's firm did us a great favor by arranging these day tours for us while he works."

Cubby saw Carmen nod in approval. He and Carmen really liked Otto and had agreed in the cab ride to do their best to enjoy themselves. It was their last day in Austria before departing for Germany the next morning to meet relatives.

Cubby turned toward the church and began to follow a small group of tourists in the direction of the main entrance as his mother and sister silently trailed behind.

Upon entering the Hofkirche, Cubby's jaw dropped. The sudden shock of stepping into another century impressed him as it did even the most casual tourist. The atmosphere was oddly quiet even for a church. He could almost feel the presence of spirits all around him. At age eleven, Cubby knew that there probably was no such thing as ghosts. But on the other hand, he thought ghosts were kind of cool, and he liked the idea they might exist. Cubby quickly returned to reality when he heard a familiar voice.

"Carmen! Cubby! How is my favorite American family this morning?" asked a smiling Otto who received their smiles in return.

"Very good to see you again, Otto," replied Friederun. "We are sorry today will be our last full day in Austria, but we are pleased to be spending at least part of it with you."

"The pleasure is mine, madam," said Otto with a slight bow.

Cubby noted that Otto was casually but neatly dressed. He wore a popular Austrian boiled wool vest, and as always, he projected a smile full of cultured European charm and humor. His English was almost perfect and reflected only the slightest accent.

Otto continued. "Well, shall we begin our tour? I can't help but notice, children, that you seem quite impressed by the structure in the center of the church. It is built from white marble and brass carvings, which are surrounded by a black and gold gate. What you see before you is known as a cenotaph. It was completed in the second half of the sixteenth century by Emperor Ferdinand I as a memorial to his grandfather, Emperor Maximilian I. However, when Emperor Maximilian died in Upper Austria in 1519, he was buried in a cathedral near Vienna in accordance with his final wishes. So this beautiful tomb is actually empty, and such a structure is known as a cenotaph. The figure seen on top of the monument represents Maximilian I, and he is facing the main altar in eternal prayer. Surrounding him are figures of the four virtues: prudence, justice, fortitude, and temperance."

"May I ask a question?" said Cubby as he shifted the small backpack he was wearing around his shoulders.

"Of course," replied Otto.

Cubby said, "What are all these statues surrounding the cenograph?"

Friederun smiled at her son. She enjoyed his active interest in the tour.

"The word is ceno*taph*!" gently but firmly injected Carmen.

She was two years older than Cubby, and it seemed to him that she delighted in correcting her younger brother at every opportunity. She also enjoyed being several inches taller, at least for the time being, and she was obviously more mature. Carmen also wore a backpack but a smaller, more stylish one.

It sometimes seemed to Cubby that his mother favored Carmen over him. Maybe it was because his sister was so good at geography, and his mom was a geography teacher in one of Chicago's better schools. But without admitting it, Cubby had learned on this trip to enjoy Carmen's company more and more despite the sometimes unspeakable nonsense younger brothers believe they have to tolerate from older sisters. And he honestly had to admit that his sister had to sometimes deal with his shenanigans as well.

"Sehr gut, Carmen, or perhaps I should say 'Very good,'" Otto said. "And I wish to observe that Cubby's eyes are as keen as Carmen's ears. There are over two dozen larger-than-life bronze statues surrounding the cenotaph, which include Maximilian I's ancestors, relatives, and favored heroes of times past. Some you may already know. Take that tall, handsome fellow right there holding a shield. Do you recognize him, Cubby?"

"No, not really, but he looks like a great knight!"

Carmen spoke again. "Cubby, it looks like I have keen eyes too. Check out the bottom of the statue."

Slowly and taking his time, Cubby deliberately and somewhat clumsily said, "Artur König v. England?"

"In my language, könig means king," Otto said.

"Oh now I get it," said Cubby. His blue eyes brightened even more than usual. "It's King Arthur from England. Wow! The one who created the Knights of the Round Table?"

"That's correct!" replied Otto. "And if you like knights, I have something very special I would like to show you and your family later in the Silver Chapel."

Friederun, who could probably pass herself off as the children's older sister, looked at her watch and interrupted. "I apologize, Otto, but it is almost noon. The children and I are supposed to meet my husband for lunch nearby."

Cubby jumped in. "Mom, could Carmen and I stay here with Otto while you meet Dad? We're having supper together later, and maybe you could just get us sandwiches?"

Carmen nodded in agreement.

"We don't want to impose on Otto," responded Friederun. "He needs a break from us and has to eat lunch as well."

"Thank you, madam, but it's no imposition at all. I actually would like the children to see the Silver Chapel in the upper level here at the *Hofkirche*. There's something unique there, and it involves a special story I would like to share with them."

"Please, please, Mom!" the children begged.

"We'll be fine, madam," Otto said. "Enjoy a private lunch with your husband. Let's just exchange handy numbers."

"Handy numbers?" asked Friederun.

"Oh I'm sorry," said Otto. "'Handy' is our nickname for a cell phone."

Friederun nodded in understanding. They exchanged numbers while Cubby and Carmen huddled.

"Carm, what do you think is in the Silver Chapel?" ty asked Cubby.

"I hope it's something romantic," Carmen whispered.

"Oh boogers!" said Cubby. He rolled his eyes.

Friederun and Otto turned to the children. She gently cautioned, "Now you two be good. I'm counting on it."

"No worries, Mom," said Carmen. "I'll keep these two fellows in line."

Friederun and Otto smiled and nodded to one another. She briefly hugged the children, turned, and exited the church with a wave as Cubby gave her a thumbs-up.

Otto clapped his hands and began to rub them together in anticipation of what was to come. "Well, are you ready for the Silver Chapel?" The children nodded their heads. "Then follow me!"

Otto walked to the rear of the church toward a marble staircase. He began to lecture amiably as they moved. "Awaiting us are the tombs of some very special people who first met in friendship and adventure. And now they remain together forever in love."

Carmen smiled broadly at her brother, but Cubby again rolled his eyes. He didn't seem too sure where Otto was leading them. They reached the church's upper level. Otto put a hand on each of their shoulders as they stood in front of a large metal grate. It covered the entire front of the chapel and ran from floor to ceiling.

"Do you see the grate? Now walk over, look through it, and tell me what you see." The children obediently strolled over to the giant grate covering the entire front of the Silver Chapel. They placed their hands on the vertical bars and peered through.

Otto remained silent as the children drank in the chapel. Then he asked, "So what do you observe?"

Cubby was transfixed by something. He spoke first. "I see a knight up on the left wall. He is on his knees praying or perhaps ..."

"...keeping watch over the beautiful lady," said Carmen finishing the sentence.

"Sehr gut!" Otto said. "And do you want to know who they were and why they are still honored after so many centuries?"

"Yes of course," said Carmen almost breathlessly.

Cubby, still wide eyed, stared at the kneeling knight and simply nodded.

"Excellent. It is my pleasure to tell you their story, but you must promise to share it one day with your children."

They eagerly shook their heads in agreement.

"Well then, Carmen. Learn now the story of Margarethe, the kingdom queen. And Cubby, hear now about a great knight, Theo, who overcame many challenges and rose from the peasant life to lofty heights. Our story begins just over nine hundred years ago in the Holy Roman Empire. The year is 1110, the beginning of the twelfth century, and the time of the High Middle Ages. The First Crusade had ended about ten years earlier. Theo's father, Josef, is about to be knighted at the kingdom castle by Good King Johann."

2

THE KINGDOM COURT AD 1110

Theo stood next to his mother, Lorraine. He was beside himself with expectation and excitement. He stared proudly at his father, Josef, standing in front of the throne with his head slightly bowed. As King Johann rose from his throne and took a few steps forward, he gazed approvingly at Josef. The king paused and looked at the assembled crowd clearly enjoying the moment and its magnificent setting. He then asked in a voice for all to hear, "Who sponsors this man for knighthood?"

"We do!"

Theo's eyes turned to Bishop Radbert Kohlhaas, who drew himself up on his crozier as he responded. "Baron von Engel and I sponsor Josef for knighthood."

The baron nodded in agreement. Theo knew from his father about the many scars and difficult challenges this unique group of four men had experienced during the crusade. Despite those struggles, they all appeared to Theo to be in the prime of their lives. Each of them was bearded and a bit taller than most, and they had that special bond among men who had fought alongside each another.

The king looked at Josef and said, "And to whom do you swear allegiance?"

"I swear allegiance to you, Majesty, and to our God in heaven," Josef said.

"Then kneel," the king said with royal formality.

Josef knelt and bowed as Bishop Kohlhaas and Baron von Engel looked on approvingly. Theo glanced up at his mother, who was beaming with pride. He looked briefly toward the other side of the Great Hall. He saw Princess Margarethe, who stood near her father, King Johann, along with her mother, Queen Annemarie. Margarethe's and Theo's eyes met briefly, and despite the seriousness of the moment, they smiled at each other. Theo realized he was closer to Princess Margarethe than he ever had been. Standing behind the princess was her best friend, Lady Marianne, who appeared totally enchanted by and absorbed in the ceremony.

King Johann drew his sword and touched Josef three times on his shoulders, right-left-right, as he intoned the ceremonial words of knighthood. "In the name of God, Saint George, and Saint Michael, I give you the right to bear arms and mete out justice. Bishop, the spurs."

The bishop and the baron moved forward and affixed spurs to Josef's armored feet.

"Arise! I dub thee a knight. And for now and evermore be recognized as Sir Josef."

Trumpets played a fanfare that almost startled Theo. Sir Josef arose, stood erect on his tall frame, and turned to the applauding audience. He smiled slightly, pursed his lips, and acknowledged the applause. Theo knew his father to be a humble man who must have been feeling great pride at that moment. King Johann stepped behind Sir Josef, placed his hands on his shoulders, and whispered something in his ear. Theo guessed it may have involved gratitude for the many lives his father had saved including the baron, the bishop, and King Johann. Sir Josef bowed his head to acknowledge the king's private tribute.

King Johann motioned Theo and his mother over and waved the crowd silent. "Sir Josef has served our kingdom and our people well for many years. Examples include his exemplary bravery during the crusade, the establishment of our military training program, and his support of the welcomed peace we now enjoy. I wish at this time to also recognize his family. I give you Lady Lorraine and their son, Theo. It is my wish that you embrace them as full members of this court. Further, with the approval of his parents, Theo will receive training as a page and then later as a squire. If he proves half the man as is his father, he too will one day be a knight of this kingdom."

The crowd applauded.

"Sire, may I make a suggestion?" asked Queen Annemarie as Princess Margarethe and Lady Marianne stood next to her. The king quickly nodded in agreement. "With your approval, may I suggest you, Baron von Engel, and Sir Josef visit the armory and view our newly anointed knight's sword and shield that Sir Ducu has specially prepared for today? I would like to speak with Lady Lorraine and invite her to an event being planned. And perhaps Bishop Kohlhaas can provide the children a brief tour of the kingdom chapel?"

King Johann surveyed all parties for approval with his eyes and said, "Splendid suggestions! Thank you, my queen."

A smiling Queen Annemarie linked arms with Lady Lorraine as she spoke to her. "You must attend our upcoming picnic to welcome spring. It will be at the lake below the castle."

"Your Majesty is too kind," responded Lady Lorraine. "Of course I will come." She looked toward her son. "And may I bring Theo?"

"Absolutely," the queen responded. "There will be several more children there."

They smiled and walked away chatting.

"Well, gentlemen, it appears we should be off to the armory," noted the king. "Dear bishop, will you be all right with the children for a short time?"

"Thank you, Majesty. I will be fine, and perhaps I can teach them something new," responded the bishop. "And sire, I will meet with you in the armory soon thereafter to finalize today's ceremony."

"Very well then," said the king. "Let us be away and reconvene again in the armory prior to the evening banquet."

King Johann, Baron von Engel, and Sir Josef departed leaving Bishop Kohlhaas alone with Princess Margarethe, Lady Marianne, and Theo who gathered around him.

"Do you all know each other?" asked the bishop.

Theo felt a bit uncomfortable. He shook his head and looked down.

"I am Princess Margarethe," stated the princess with the confidence of a queen. "And this is my dearest friend, Lady Marianne."

Theo looked at them as they stared waiting for him to say something. Both girls were about ten, the same as Theo. They all were born not long after the end of the crusade after their fathers had returned home from battle.

Theo felt the bishop gently nudge him with his crozier. "Speak your name, boy, and introduce yourself properly to these young ladies."

"My name is Theo … it's Theo," he said quietly, his eyes to the floor. *At least I didn't stutter,* he thought. *That would have been too embarrassing especially in front of the princess.* Theo suddenly wanted nothing more than to impress her. But he told himself something like that might be impossible for someone like him.

"Try again, boy," the bishop said. "This time with eyes up and a bow to the ladies."

Theo looked up slowly, took a breath, and ratcheted up his courage. "I am Theo, son of—" He paused and then happily said, "—Sir Josef and Lady Lorraine." He promptly bowed to the young ladies while looking up for approval from Bishop Kohlhaas, who validated the effort with a slight, silent nod.

Marianne said, "Theo," with a smile.

Princess Margarethe repeated, "Theo," but with a bit more emphasis.

Theo looked directly at the girls. He smiled at Marianne, beamed at the princess, felt himself turning red, and dropped his gaze to the ground while shuffling his feet. He looked to the bishop as if for further instruction.

Bishop Kohlhaas rolled his eyes. "Good. Introductions are complete. Let's be off to the chapel."

The girls ran ahead while the bishop grabbed Theo's shoulder. "Lesson one, boy. Faint heart never won fair lady. Always remember, Fortuna audaces iuvat." He noted Theo's perplexity. "That is Latin for 'Fortune favors the bold.' Make that lesson two." The bishop gave Theo a gentle nudge forward.

Elsewhere deep in the castle, King Johann, Baron von Engel, and Sir Josef reached the armory. Sir Josef looked on as two guards snapped to attention while Sir Ducu, the master-at-arms, approached the trio. "Welcome, Your Majesty," he stated as he produced keys for the armory door.

Sir Ducu had fought in the crusade, and a patch over his left eye attested to the fact he had been wounded. He was not a large man, but his abilities as a craftsman and a warrior were well respected. "I expect you are here to see the shield and sword prepared for our newest knight?" Sir Ducu turned and bowed respectfully to Sir Josef, who had every expectation he would be pleased by the master-at-arm's efforts. In 1099, during the siege of Jerusalem, Sir Josef had saved Sir Ducu's life during the final major attack of the crusade.

The four entered the armory, which was filled with a great variety of weaponry and armor. Swords and broadswords neatly lined the walls along with war hammers, battle-axes, and several types of flanged maces. Several suits of armor were free standing and placed throughout the armory.

In addition to his skills with metal, Sir Ducu prided himself with the armor-related items of clothing he designed. His creations were known throughout the kingdom. One was the gambeson, which was typically worn under the metal shell to make the upper armor itself more comfortable for the wearer. Sir Ducu was also credited with the invention of the surcoat, which was worn over the armor. It was made of long, lightweight material with a loose, split skirt and a red cross depicted on the front. It was particularly popular among the Knights Templar and had become a quintessential part of a knight's appearance.

"Look here!" noted Baron von Engel as he pointed to a shiny sword and shield in the center of the room. "They are magnificent!"

"Magnificent!" echoed King Johann.

Sir Josef looked upon his new sword and shield.

He was transfixed.

"Are you pleased?" Sir Ducu earnestly asked Sir Josef.

A few seconds passed in silence until Sir Josef spoke. "Well done, Ducu." He reached out his hand to Sir Ducu's shoulder and squeezed it tightly for a moment. "Very well done!"

Sir Josef noted emotion in Sir Ducu's leathery face as his lips tightened into a smile.

King Johann and the baron clapped Ducu on the back to mark their approval of his hard work and the results.

"We await the arrival of Bishop Kohlhaas," said the king. "He will bless the sword and shield and conduct a final ceremony."

"In that case," responded Ducu, "I will excuse myself and leave the armory to Your Majesty."

Sir Ducu walked to the door as the baron trailed behind. Sir Josef noted the baron congratulated Ducu one more time on his work and closed the door to give the remaining three some privacy.

Picking up his new sword, Sir Josef ran his finger up and down along one side of the blade and spoke. "It is magnificent, isn't it?" He turned over the blade and smiled broadly when he saw the cross of the Knights Templar etched into the metal.

The bishop and the children arrived at the kingdom chapel. Theo was paying close attention to everyone and everything.

"This is the house of God," intoned Bishop Kohlhaas. "But it is also a place where people can come to learn as well as worship. May I ask, Theo, if you can read and write?"

"Only a little, Your Eminence. My parents are trying to teach me. They are also learning," responded Theo.

"That is more than most. One reason we have art in the chapel in the form of painting and sculptures is because most people can neither write nor read. Pictures and images help give them an understanding of and an appreciation for our faith. For example, do you three see that stained glass window there?" The children looked toward the window and nodded. "What story from the Bible do you think it represents?"

"I believe it is Adam and Eve in the Garden of Eden," said the princess.

"Quite close," responded the bishop. "It is indeed Adam with the first woman God created. But her name was Lilith. Eve was actually Adam's second wife."

"Really?" asked Lady Marianne. "I thought with Adam there was only Eve."

Bishop Kohlhaas continued. "It is an interesting story that is addressed by multiple religions, not just Christianity. Basically, Adam and Lilith were created from the earth's soil. But over time, Lilith displeased both God and Adam. She would utter God's name out loud, which was considered disrespectful. And since she had been created from the same earth as Adam had been, she refused to be in any way subservient to him. That led ... to conflict. As a result, Lilith was banished by God from the garden. She is often portrayed with a human head and a serpent's body. Then God proceeded to create Eve from Adam himself ... from Adam's rib as you may have heard."

"What became of Lilith?" asked Theo.

"Ahh, that's rather interesting," noted the bishop. "The legend states that God decided to give her eternal life to soften her banishment from Eden." The bishop smiled to himself and began walking away. He stopped, turned, and said, "Some say she still wanders the earth."

Theo and Lady Marianne's eyes widened. They looked at each other a bit confused and afraid as the bishop began to lead them to another area in the chapel. But as they were walking behind the bishop, Princess Margarethe whispered, "I think Lilith was punished a bit too much for wanting to be treated the same as Adam." Lady Marianne shrugged with a bit of uncertainty, but Theo stared thoughtfully at the princess. He knew she was no silly girl. Despite her young age, she was a person to be treated with respect and deference. He immediately liked that about her.

"Now let's continue our tour to something very new," said the bishop. "It is a symbol of the cross and a special knighthood that was recently and formally approved by our holy father in Rome. It represents the Knights Templar, a special group of men formed at the end of the crusade. These knights are Christendom's finest warriors. They were originally created to protect pilgrims traveling to Jerusalem following the victory in the crusade a decade ago. Up to this very day, there is a group of Templars stationed in Jerusalem. Other groups of Templars are strategically placed in various locations to support and maintain the goals of this unique fraternity of knights."

"How do men find and join the Knights Templar?" asked Theo.

"They will find you," responded the bishop. "That's lesson three for today. Now let us look at one other item. Princess Margarethe, do you know who this statue over here represents?"

After thinking a bit, she slowly responded. "I believe, Eminence ... I believe it represents St. Boniface."

"Correct," noted the bishop with extra pleasure in his voice. "And you may recall that he is the eighth-century saint credited with the use of a tree to celebrate the birth of Christ. Remember that we place one each year in the castle courtyard to celebrate His nativity. But do you also see the symbol on his cross?"

"I do," responded Marianne. "It looks like two circles joined in the middle. What does it mean?"

The bishop nodded knowingly and stated, "There are those who say the symbol means something like 'forever.' Others say it represents the eternal love God has for us. There is neither a beginning nor an end."

He traced the symbol in the air with a finger.

"Could it mean the love we have for one another?" asked Princess Margarethe as she also drew the symbol in the air.

"I imagine it could," responded Bishop Kohlhaas as he grabbed his beard in thought. "But I believe it is primarily intended to demonstrate more-divine and universal truths."

"For me," said the princess, "it will be a symbol that love is forever." She looked at Theo, who did not avert his eyes this time.

"Think of it as you wish," the bishop said.

Marianne smiled at the discussion. Smiling was something that had been rare for her until only recently. Her father, an earl and a veteran of the crusade, had passed away several months earlier from pneumonia. Her mother had died from complications during childbirth. King Johann insisted Marianne move to the castle under his protection. She and the princess had been inseparable ever since.

"So enough education for now," declared Bishop Kohlhaas. "Come, children. King Johann and others await me in the armory. Let's be off to the great hall where I must deliver you for the evening's fest. And be mindful not to stay too late tonight. Tomorrow will be the picnic at the kingdom lake."

The next day, the sun warmed the morning and shone on the lake below the castle. Before joining the other children, Theo had responded to his mother's request to help organize the royal tent. It had been pitched next to the lake, and it housed the day's food and games. The announcement bell, recently painted red, stood ready for use when it was time for the formal programs to begin.

Theo was getting a bit anxious to join the other children who were playing in the nearby field. He listened as Queen Annemarie and his mother, Lady Lorraine, discussed the day and learned that four of the king's guards were posted in various locations around the lake for safety. There had been reports of activity in the area involving men who sought to kidnap women and children for sale into slavery. One rumor was that a band of Saracen marauders was scouring the countryside and would do anything for gold. Their leader was a ruthless and daring young Saracen named Faruk.

However, Queen Annemarie displayed a sense of calm and peace. The castle and the guards were all close at hand. The queen surveyed the scene, looked at the children having fun, and spoke to Lady Lorraine. "They are playing nicely, and we should have an abundance of food and games for them to enjoy. Your help and that of the other ladies of the court is most appreciated," she said.

"It is very much my pleasure," Lady Lorraine said. "The past few days have been remarkable. Your kindness and the king's ... my husband and I shall never forget it. And I've never seen Theo happier," she noted as she turned toward her son.

The queen smiled. "Theo, I think it's time for you to join the other children. And thank you for your help this morning."

Theo bowed slightly and looked to his mother, who was smiling and nodding her approval. That was all Theo needed. He rapidly ran off to meet up with the others a short distance away.

He joined an ongoing game of tag with Princess Margarethe, Lady Marianne, and a pack of other children. After a few moments, one of the girls chased around a group with the princess among them. Theo was cheering them on when suddenly Princess Margarethe tripped and fell. He ran to help her up. She said, "I'm fine," but she blushed as Theo lifted her by her arm. He didn't know why, but he liked it when he held the princess and helped her to her feet. The other children returned to their game since all appeared to be well.

Theo slowly let go of her hand. The princess brushed herself off. Theo was turning toward the other children when she blurted out, "Theo!" He stopped and looked at her. After searching for something to say, the princess said, "That was very good of you to help me. It was ... chivalrous."

"My pleasure, Your Highness," Theo responded with a slight bow. Before he turned back toward the lake, he thought he saw Princess Margarethe smile as she rubbed her hand and elbow he had just touched in a simple act of kindness. Theo walked ahead and smiled as well. He realized at that very moment that he was happier than he had ever been. He had no way of knowing it was all about to change.

He looked in the vicinity of the royal tent and the red bell. As he continued forward to the lake, he could see the reflection of the castle on the water and thought to himself, *How peaceful!* He looked back at the group of playing children and saw Princess Margarethe and Lady Marianne laughing and smiling. He turned his gaze to the tent and observed his mother and Queen Annemarie in conversation.

Suddenly, the relative calm was broken when he heard a flock of birds break the stillness with rapid flapping of their wings. Theo sensed something was wrong. Although he was unaware, a lone arrow had just arched through the air and struck a guard at the far edge of the lake. Then a few seconds later, another arrow hit the guard stationed near the announcement bell. Theo saw him tumble backward near the royal tent.

"Run to the castle!" Theo shouted to the princess and the other children, who began to scream. "Run!" He sped to his mother and the queen, who both slowly began to realize the danger. "Lead everyone to the castle! Now! Now!" he shouted.

Theo spotted a band of marauders emerging from the forest in the distance as they appeared across the lake. He raced to the bell and pounded it with the mallet hanging there for that purpose. He turned toward the tent and saw the queen leading everyone to the castle. Two guards appeared and flashed past Theo on their way to engage the invaders.

Unbeknownst to Theo, Lady Lorraine was directly behind the guards running to her son. She intuitively sought to protect Theo as she continued forward toward the clanging bell. Looking right, she saw a Saracen marauder suddenly appear from behind a tree. He began to run straight at Theo before he suddenly stopped, carefully aimed his crossbow, and fired. Just as Theo sensed Lady Lorraine's presence, she instinctively threw herself in front of him and was struck by the arrow. Theo fell to his knees next to his mother, shook her, and cried "Mutti! Mutti!"

Alerted by the bell, knights raced from the castle and toward the lake as the queen, her ladies, and the children ran into the castle. Sir Josef, Baron von Engel, and four companion knights rushed past the queen to join the battle by the lake.

The two remaining guards took up a protective position near Theo, who was sobbing and grasping his mother. Other marauders joined the Saracen bowman and surged forward to the bell area. A sword fight ensued. Four of the enemy were cut down by the two guards, who fought until they were themselves mortally wounded.

After hanging back from the hand-to-hand fighting, the Saracen with the crossbow reloaded his weapon and took point-blank aim at the boy. Theo stared at him with intense hatred. A knife silently hurtled through the air and struck the Saracen in the throat. Sir Josef had thrown it.

From a safe distance and on higher ground, Faruk, the leader of the marauders, held a crossbow as he watched the battle by the lake unfold. Despite his relative youth, Faruk had experienced victory and defeat in battle many times. He was driven by a lust for gold, which conflicted with the notion of living to fight another day.

Sir Josef, the baron, and their companion knights charged the final group of marauders until they made actual contact. They fought them to the death. The knights proved to be lethal and made short work of the remaining invaders, who all appeared to be Saracens.

As the last few enemies fled back to the forest, Theo saw his father looking at him. Sir Josef quickly came to Theo and his mother. "God in heaven! Lorraine!"

"She saved me, Father. And now so have you," Theo said through his tears.

"Theo, my son," uttered Sir Josef. "Was it you who sounded the alarm and saved so many today?" Theo nodded. His father continued, "I am so proud of—" A whish and a thud. Sir Josef was struck from behind by an arrow and was instantly silenced. He crumpled and fell next to the body of Lady Lorraine.

Baron von Engel spun around in all directions but saw no source of the arrow. He knelt over Sir Josef's body and drank in the enormity of the situation. The baron gently touched his old friend's shoulder as he bit his lip. He again surveyed the scene and looked down at Theo, who was stunned.

"Courage, Theo, courage. These brave guards and your good parents saved you as you have undoubtedly saved others by sounding the alarm." The baron paused. "I have no son, but if you agree, I vow to raise you as if you were my own."

Theo looked at him. But he was still in shock.

A large party on horseback arrived from the castle. King Johann quickly dismounted and walked to Theo as Baron von Engel stood, bowed, and pointed at the bell area. The king grimly took in the situation. His eyes moistened as he saw Sir Josef and Lady Lorraine next to one another. He knelt by Theo, wordlessly took him in his arms, and embraced him. Theo began to cry bitter tears as the king held back his own.

Faruk disgustedly shook his head and waved off the rest of his men. He was the one who had taken deliberate aim with his crossbow while down on one knee and had looked on dispassionately as the arrow found its mark—the tall knight. He turned to leave almost as unhappy with the loss of his men as he was with their lack of success. Next time—if there ever was a next time—he would be more prepared and increase the size of his force. It was hard for him to fathom that his raiding plan had been foiled by what appeared to be a boy and a bell.

As he watched the kingdom's men and horses depart the tent area, Faruk thought about the day's events and his life. He hadn't always been someone who preyed on others. He had been raised an orphan near the border of Turkey and Syria. It had been his misfortune to fall in with older boys who had already taken the wrong path. Though he never spoke of it, he knew he had been born on the wrong side of the bed. There were whispers that his father was Kilij Arslan I, the sultan of Rum. He knew nothing of his mother.

Necessity had forced Faruk into the life of a pickpocket, and he rapidly evolved into a warrior-thief. He was a natural-born leader who cut an imposing figure; his countrymen needed little incentive to follow him wherever he led. But he was intelligent and knew the life he was living could not go on forever.

He waved over two of his men, Rami the Marksman and Nijad the Tall. They were brothers. Faruk spoke. "It has been a bad day for us but also for the infidels. Gather the rest of the men and let us rethink our strategy. We must find other areas to raid that offer less resistance."

The brothers nodded and departed toward the forest. Faruk looked down at the lake. He wondered if he would ever return.

The next day, a funeral service was held in the kingdom chapel. Twin coffins were centered near the altar, and four others containing the king's guards were spread out in the chapel. Through his shock and disbelief, Theo looked on as Bishop Kohlhaas blessed the coffins with smoking incense. Its semisweet smell permeated the room.

The king and queen sat on either side of Theo in the left-front pew. Next to them were Princess Margarethe and Lady Marianne. Sitting in the right-front pew was Duke Teufelmund. He was from a neighboring kingdom and was a ward of King Johann since childhood. To the duke's right sat Baron von Engel.

The bishop handed off the incense thurible to an assistant and walked through the smoke to the front of the chapel. Theo and all present listened as the bishop spoke. "The events of yesterday morning have left us all deeply saddened. But we can take comfort from the words 'No greater love,' which were exemplified by Christ crucified for us all. Those same words also describe our kingdom guards who gave their lives to protect women and children. The final gift Sir Josef and Lady Lorraine gave their son was the ultimate example of love by laying down their lives for him. And in the knightly traditions of bravery and unselfishness, young Theo himself sounded the alarm that saved many including our beloved Queen Annemarie."

The queen and the princess turned to Theo, who sat silently and stared at the altar.

"King Johann has given me permission to say that one day, Theo, when you have come of age, you are to be knighted as your father before you. Until then, you will remain under the protection of the kingdom with Baron von Engel as your mentor and teacher."

Theo bowed.

Bishop Kohlhaas motioned all to stand. He raised and opened his arms while intoning in Latin, "Requiescant in pace." He blessed all in the chapel and said, "In nomine Patris, et Filii, et Spiritus Sancti."

All in the chapel responded, "Amen."

The silent congregation slowly and respectfully began to file out. Theo sat and waited with the royal party a few moments in his private sorrow before standing and crossing in front of the king while exiting the royal pew. Theo walked between his parents' coffins and touched each of them. From behind, the bishop silently gave him a blessing.

Duke Teufelmund approached Theo. "Theo, I am Duke Teufelmund. I wish to express my profound sorrow to you. I also lost my parents when I was about your age. I wish you strength." He turned and departed down the center aisle of the chapel.

Despite the solemnity of the moment and the strong aroma of incense, Theo noticed a terrible smell. He realized that the duke had the worst breath of anyone he had ever met. But that day it did not matter. Nothing really mattered.

Baron von Engel approached and placed his hand on Theo's shoulder. "We will talk later."

As the baron moved toward the rear of the chapel, Princess Margarethe walked up to Theo. Without speaking, she discreetly took his left hand and pressed a piece of paper into it. She tenderly kissed him on the cheek, turned, and looked directly at the statue of St. Boniface. Theo stood still and was all but numb. Without looking at it, he placed the paper in his pocket and took a deep breath. He exhaled, looked left and right, and touched the coffins one last time.

3

Innsbruck, Austria
Present Day

Otto paused telling his story and looked very seriously at Carmen and Cubby.

With tears in her eyes, Carmen said, "Poor Theo. What a sad story, Otto."

"It is sad," replied Otto. "But there is a great deal more to tell. Plus, I imagine you might have some questions."

"Of course!" Cubby said. "Will Theo really become a knight? Did any more Saracen raids take place? And the Knights Templar?"

"And what becomes of Theo and Princess Margarethe? And was that story about the Garden of Eden and Lilith really true?" Carmen asked.

"I know there are many questions," responded Otto. "But time demands that I continue our story. So let me answer just one question from each of you before moving on."

"Okay," said Cubby. "Who was this Duke Teufelmund who was at the funeral?"

Otto responded. "Duke Teufelmund was from a very noble family that had fallen on hard times due to a terrible event. When he was a child, his parents and many others perished when a flash flood destroyed their castle, which was in a valley. Young Teufelmund was sleeping in the uppermost floor of the castle and was spared. He was rescued the next morning by a few village fishermen who rowed out to the castle in a small boat. They took him to his only living family member, an uncle, who had a singular reputation for brutality.

"After only a few months of misery and discomfort for both, the uncle gave his unhappy and troublesome nephew over to a monastery, where he was quietly raised for many years. The monks did their best to instruct him in Christian values in keeping with their beliefs and his nobility, but the loss of his family coupled with the cruelty of his uncle had damaged him greatly. Without any family or friends, he trusted no one but himself.

"Good King Johann learned of the tragedy from a monk passing through the kingdom while returning from a pilgrimage to Jerusalem. The king had met Duke Teufelmund's parents some years earlier at a marriage fest, and given the circumstances and his noble lineage, he decided to take young Teufelmund under his protection. Will that explanation suffice?"

Cubby nodded.

"And what do you wish to know, Carmen?"

She responded, "I've been thinking of what you told us and do have a question that must be answered."

"And what would that be?" Otto replied.

"Why ... the note the princess gave Theo of course. What was in it?" she asked.

"Ah" said Otto. "The note. It was something Theo carried with him all his remaining days. It contained no words but was simply a symbol. When Theo finally dug the note from his pocket and looked at it later that terrible day, it began to lift his heavy heart from the darkness back into the light."

The children looked at Otto with wide eyes and open mouths. They were frantic for a clearer explanation. Otto of course understood. He took out a pen from his vest pocket and drew something on his palm.

Carmen grabbed Otto's hand and opened it for her and Cubby to see. And what she saw was the symbol for infinity that Otto had described earlier from the cross of St. Boniface in the kingdom chapel. Carmen looked content.

"So," declared Otto, "it's time for me to ask you two a question. Do you know what it means?"

Cubby was thinking hard. He scratched his head and said, "Well, I'm not really sure."

Carmen hesitated but smiled broadly. "Of course! It's the symbol for infinity. And Princess Margarethe was telling Theo she loved him and that she would do so forever!"

"Precisely!" Otto said as Cubby gave a thumbs-up. "You are a bright girl and have been paying close attention. Shall I continue?"

Carmen and Cubby nodded in excited anticipation.

Otto resumed his narration. "About ten years passed, and there was relative peace. Life was lived as it was meant to be. That was until another and much more dangerous threat arose for the kingdom."

4

THE KINGDOM CASTLE AD 1120

Princess Margarethe entered the balcony and watched as the kingdom's knights and nobles completed their daily training in the castle courtyard. Duke Teufelmund had the reputation as the best swordsman in the kingdom, and he seemed to excel during these training sessions. The squires, who always watched the duke fight, began their exercises once the first session was completed. A dozen young squires brandishing wooden swords took up fighting positions. They commenced their training in preparation for potential combat.

The princess looked on from above with eyes for only one. Squire Theo was fighting fiercely and vanquishing his training partner, young Squire Michael. Theo cast a glance in the princess's direction; he paid a stiff penalty for that distraction with a blow to the head delivered by Squire Michael's wooden sword.

The princess gasped as she saw Theo fall to one knee. She saw Baron von Engel approach him with an obvious look of disapproval. She was a distance away but close enough to hear his chastisements.

"Theo!" shouted the baron. "Use your head for something other than a target for your opponent's sword. Stay focused on the fight.

Look left with your eyes but move right with your body. Do not allow your enemy to anticipate your every move. And do not ever allow yourself to be distracted in combat!"

The baron cast a glance at the princess, who saw Theo nod to the baron, stand, and motion for his partner to continue the training.

Duke Teufelmund, who appeared refreshed—unlike someone who had just completed heavy training—appeared on the balcony and approached Princess Margarethe. He would no doubt try again to curry her favor as he had unsuccessfully done several times before. The duke greeted her pleasantly. "How is Your Highness today?"

"I am well," she responded with a polite smile. She returned to looking at the training and began inching herself away from the duke and his offensive breath.

Duke Teufelmund remained silent, but the princess suspected that his desire to win her favor was a clumsy attempt to garner support for some future plan. Bad breath aside, she well knew his reputation for ungentlemanly conduct toward the servants. Lady Marianne and the princess often had discussed the duke's lack of chivalry and non-existent empathy for others. His faults outweighed even his prowess with a sword.

Turning to view the courtyard and staring out to mimic the princess, the duke tried to restart a conversation. "What do you think of Baron von Engel?"

The princess looked at him quizzically.

"I mean, Your Highness, I don't understand how he came to be in service to this kingdom. I know he fought in the crusade and has served the king many years, but I never hear him speak of his home."

"That is because he considers the kingdom his home. Baron von Engel and the king saved each other's lives in the crusade when they were younger men," noted the princess. "The baron's father was a great knight who died after a long illness at his castle while his son was fighting in Jerusalem. Not long thereafter, the baron's remaining family was murdered by a band of rogues and thieves. His castle and estates were ransacked and destroyed. This turned a joyful return into a tragedy when Baron von Engel, still accompanied by my father, returned to his ancestral home from the crusade some twenty years ago. When they and their companion knights learned what happened, my father proposed that they track down those responsible.

"They quickly found the villains, who promptly met their

deserved fate. The undisciplined band of thieves was no match for the battle-tested swords of the crusaders. After justice was dispensed, my father proposed to the baron that they remain together in friendship and as comrades in arms. My father has made it a practice to help those in need as you well know, Your Grace."

Duke Teufelmund paused, bowed slightly, and then replied, "Indeed I do, Your Highness."

The princess turned back to the training in progress when Bishop Kohlhaas hurriedly walked up to them. "Highness, your mother asks that you join her in her chambers. There is important news."

Princess Margarethe observed that the bishop was looking concerned but could not discern any particular reaction from the duke. She simply nodded to them, cast one more look at Theo, and departed for her mother's chambers.

"My Lord Bishop," stated the duke. "May I share something with you in confidence?"

"Of course, Your Grace," responded Bishop Kohlhaas.

"There is something about Baron von Engel that sets off warning signals with me. I can't say with certainty what bothers me, but I'm not sure he can be trusted," flatly stated the duke.

The bishop, already looking distracted since his arrival, raised his eyebrows, and his eyes grew cold. "I would share these thoughts with no one else, Your Grace. For now, there are more serious matters that will require all the strength and attention we can muster. The news we received today is news of war. There is a new Saracen threat to the kingdom. We must quickly form an army and prepare for battle. Does the king have your support?"

"Of course," replied the duke. "Of course!"

A short time later, a serious-looking Princess Margarethe entered the courtyard with Lady Marianne. They paused by the castle well. Theo, who had just finished the day's training, looked exhausted but nodded to the princess and Lady Marianne as he walked nearby. The princess motioned him over. She silently signaled with her eyes to Lady Marianne to give her some privacy with Theo.

"Highness," said Theo with a slight bow.

"Squire Theo," responded the princess. "You look tired and a bit injured from the training."

"Not at all, Your Highness. It is but a daily necessity to protect the kingdom."

"Indeed. More than you may know. May I share some news with you?"

Theo nodded his injured head, which had a large red knot on it above a trickle of blood.

The princess continued. "I've just left the queen. She learned a short time ago from my father that we can expect to go to war soon."

Theo's eyes opened slightly. His countenance became serious. He stood more erect. "Please continue, Highness."

"Word has reached us that the Saracens have formed an army and plan to invade and plunder our lands. They are led by Faruk the Assassin, possibly the same marauder who attacked us years ago and caused the death of... so many." She noted that Theo's nostrils flared, his eyes darkened, as his face flushed. "My father and the kingdom will need your support," noted the princess as she put a hand on his shoulder.

Theo stood straight and rigid. "King Johann and the kingdom will have my support now and always. It is my desire as well as my duty," Theo said as he looked directly at Princess Margarethe. "Forgive me, Highness, but I must excuse myself and begin to prepare. Baron von Engel will be looking for me as well as the other squires."

"There's something else, Theo. Despite this new threat, my mother reminded me today that I have been remiss in my royal duties. There is a need for me to marry soon. And she emphasized that both tradition and custom demand..." Her voice trailed off. "... that I marry a nobleman."

Theo blanched. He paused to pull himself together. His lower lip slightly quivered as he almost whispered, "I ... I ... understand."

"Theo," she said with all the love she could muster, "you must know my heart. You must know how I—"

"Highness! I ask you allow me to go prepare. I beg your leave."

Theo began to walk away but stopped, reached into his shirt, and yanked something out. He turned to Princess Margarethe. She saw he was holding a small bag. He abruptly handed it to her and rushed away without another word.

Lady Marianne walked back to the princess, who was in obvious distress. "What is the matter?"

Princess Margarethe looked at her questioningly with tears in her eyes. She opened the bag and pulled out a scrap of paper. On it was the infinity sign of St. Boniface, the one she had given Theo years earlier at his parents' funeral. She began to weep deeply as Lady Marianne hugged her tightly.

A few days later, Theo was actively involved as King Johann met with his key advisors and knights in the great hall. They had finalized their battle plans following much discussion. Maps peppered the walls and tables. The king sat on a wooden throne atop a small stage. Fortune had allowed Theo to keep himself busy since his discussion with the princess. His mind was on the business of war, but his heart ached. He looked up from a map he was studying as the king rose from the throne to address the assembly.

"Then it is agreed," the king said. "Based on our scouting reports from Baron von Engel and Squire Theo, the enemy situation is confirmed. It involves a group of roughly seventy-five marauders led by Faruk the Assassin. We will send out a primary force of a hundred personnel composed of knights and foot soldiers to bring the fight to them rather than wait for them to attack. Duke Teufelmund will act as the force commander with Baron von Engel as his deputy. Their mission is to defeat the enemy by whatever means necessary and to such an extent that they are rendered harmless to the kingdom and our people. Duke Teufelmund?"

The duke continued the briefing. "Our hope is to surprise the enemy in their encampment which, based on the scouting report, is approximately a three hours' ride from here. On my command, we will send a primary force into their center while two teams of a dozen men each encircle their camp. One team will be led by Baron von Engel. And the other team leader? Do you wish to make the announcement, Your Majesty?"

"Indeed I do, Your Grace," responded the king. "Squire Theo, step forward!"

Theo flushed, looked left and right, and stepped slowly but deliberately toward King Johann. "Yes Majesty," he responded as he stared directly into the king's eyes.

"Squire Theo," began the king. "You have well served our kingdom and this king on more than one occasion. You are your father's son, and you have made us all proud. Duty calls us now. We cannot stand on full ceremony as allowed in better times."

To follow at least a modicum of custom, King Johann looked out at the assembled group as Queen Annemarie, Princess Margarethe, and Lady Marianne entered the room. He acknowledged their presence with a smiling gaze and asked in a booming voice, "Who sponsors this man for knighthood?"

Bishop Radbert Kohlhaas lifted his head and responded, "I do!"

"And I," Baron von Engel firmly stated as he took a step forward.

The king looked at Theo. "And to whom do you swear allegiance?"

Theo, feeling somewhat in shock, recovered himself and looked directly at King Johann. "I swear allegiance to you, Majesty, and to our God in heaven."

"Then kneel," stated the king.

Theo knelt and bowed as Bishop Kohlhaas, Baron von Engel, and those assembled looked on as the king drew his sword and touched Theo three times on his shoulders, right-left-right, as he intoned the words of knighthood. "In the name of God, St. George, and St. Michael, I give you the right to bear arms and mete out justice. Baron ... the spurs."

Baron von Engel stepped forward with the spurs he and Bishop Kohlhaas affixed to Theo's feet.

The king gazed down with approval as he continued. "Arise a knight and for now and evermore be recognized as Sir Theo."

All those assembled pounded the floor and tables in approval.

Sir Theo, eyes glistening, stood and bowed to the king, Queen Annemarie, and Princess Margarethe. Bishop Kohlhaas congratulated Sir Theo, who suddenly felt himself spun in another direction. Baron von Engel had grabbed his arms. He proudly said, "My son."

As the king patted him on the back, Sir Theo noticed Duke Teufelmund standing in the corner with a blank expression. The duke then looked away and departed the room as the others came forward to congratulate Sir Theo including the queen, the princess, and Lady Marianne.

King Johann spoke. "We will celebrate well another day. But for now, I ask you to rest easy tonight. At dawn tomorrow, we must answer the call to arms."

Alone in his room, Sir Theo was having a hard time trying to sleep. The night before certain battle seemed to call more for serious reflection than the pride of being made a knight. His thoughts flooded him with multiple emotions. In his mind's eye, he saw his parents. Then there was Princess Margarethe and their impossible union. He thought of the baron, the bishop, and all those who had taught and supported him.

As he finally drifted to sleep, a cloud appeared in his dreams and slowly revealed a dark, faceless figure. Theo reasoned that it must be the Saracen who had caused devastation so many years earlier. But he knew the situation was well beyond vengeance for the loss of his parents. The kingdom and many of its people had suffered at the hands of Faruk. He was a knight and had to think like one. Justice was more important than personal revenge. He tried to push the black thoughts out of his mind.

Theo finally fell into a slumber, but it proved more fitful than restful.

5

Innsbruck, Austria
Present Day

Otto was abruptly interrupted in his narration.

"Wait, wait, wait!" implored Cubby. "Things are not going well at all." He looked at Carmen. "This is not going the way I thought it would."

"I understand," Otto said calmly. "There are highs and lows to any good story."

"And this is the low?" asked Carmen.

"One of them," Otto said.

"There's more?" Cubby asked with eyes wide.

Otto made a neutral expression with his face. "We can stop here if you wish. I mean if it's not interesting or too intense for you," Otto said.

"Are you serious?" Cubby said.

"You can't be serious!" echoed Carmen.

"Okay," responded Otto soothingly. "But try to hold your questions. Many if not all will be answered. We don't have much time left to complete the whole story."

"I think it's way cool that Theo became a knight," Cubby said. He stood, put on his sunglasses, started making circles with his arms, and said, "He's bad. He's bad. That's right. Sir Theo's a knight. Those Saracens are in trouble city. Well all right, all right, all right!"

Carmen rolled her eyes and interrupted her brother's outburst. "Otto, I must ask you a question."

Otto smiled at Cubby as he sat and gave Carmen his attention.

"Now that Sir Theo has been knighted, will that make him a member of nobility and allow him to marry Princess Margarethe?"

"Unfortunately, the answer to your question is no. During medieval times, a knight was not a noble, and neither could he expect to marry into royalty."

Carmen looked dejected, but Cubby had calmed down and then injected himself.

"Another question, Otto. What's up with this Duke Teufelmund? He's been treated so well by King Johann but doesn't seem to like anyone. And put in command of the army? Why would the king do that?"

Otto nodded. "The king had little choice but to select Duke Teufelmund to lead the army. He was the highest-ranking noble after the king, but he was a troubled soul as previously discussed. The duke was easily jealous of anyone in the king's favor. You must remember that he had lost his family at an early age and had been ill treated by a rough uncle who scarred him for life. Then he was given to monks until King Johann effectively adopted him. While grateful for the kingdom's protection, the duke favored power." Otto made a fist. "That was one thing he fully comprehended. In his mind, it provided him control over his circumstances. Despite the best efforts of the monks and others, he had almost no sense of honor or fair play ... and little or no understanding of concepts such as kindness or love. The death of his parents had affected him deeply and shaped his personality. Teufelmund preferred self-preservation and influence much more than friendship or feeling. I expect that he didn't even like himself."

"Okay," said Cubby with minimal sympathy. "Okay. But that still doesn't explain the bad breath." He made a yucky face. "Please go on, Otto. Tell us about the battle."

Carmen, who was wringing her hands a bit, nodded in agreement.

"With pleasure," stated Otto with a knowing smile. "Morning came, the task force departed the castle, and after a few hours, they drew close to the Saracen camp."

6

The Kingdom Forest AD 1120

A Saracen sentry high in a tree saw the kingdom task force approaching. He drew an arrow and fired a warning to another sentry, who signaled still another sentry in the same way. That continued with multiple sentries. Moments later, a final warning arrow struck a target near the tent where Faruk was meeting with his subordinate leaders.

Faruk continued to speak calmly as he heard the arrow land and casually turned to confirm it with his eyes. "Our sentries have just reported that the infidel task force approaches from the north. We must prepare to meet them."

Rami the Marksman spoke. "What are your orders?"

Faruk thought for a moment and then provided his directions. "Take your brother, Nijad, and eight of your best fighters. Hide near the north entrance of our camp. Don't allow yourselves to be seen until the main enemy force fully enters our tent area. Let them think they have surprised us. Once the last enemy passes the perimeter, attack from the rear and cut off any retreat. The rest of us will fight them from the other sides."

Rami bowed to Faruk and motioned to his brother, Nijad the Tall, to follow him.

A few miles away from the Saracen camp, Sir Theo saw Duke Teufelmund at the front of the column as he and Baron von Engel rode up after scouting the area. The duke was speaking with Sir Udo, the captain of the guards.

"What is the enemy situation?" asked the duke as Theo and the baron approached.

"They are still quietly in their camp," answered Baron von Engel. "I hope we still have surprise on our side, but I doubt it if these brigands are anything like their Saracen brothers in the Holy Land."

"Then we will continue as planned," said the duke.

"Yes, Your Grace," responded Sir Theo. "Since it is critical that we deploy our forces simultaneously to take advantage of whatever leverage we may have with our three-pronged attack, may I make a suggestion?"

The duke and baron nodded in agreement as Sir Theo dismounted and pulled a red cloth from his saddlebag. He tore it in two and handed one piece to the baron. "The baron and I will use these red banners to signal we are ready. We will wave them once we are in position east and west of the camp," Sir Theo stated with emphasis.

"As previously discussed, we will leave an opening at the camp's south end for a few of the marauders to retreat. They will fight all the harder if they feel they are completely surrounded," noted the baron with a voice of experience.

"Very well," responded the duke. "I will take the lead and mount a charge directly through the camp's center once I see your red signal flags. Long live the king!"

"Long live the king," responded all the men. The baron and Sir Theo snapped their horses' reins and signaled their men to follow.

Theo and the baron rode together, but only the baron spoke. "If anything goes amiss, you and I must reassemble and revise the plan. The duke and many in the main force are untested in battle," said the baron. "I will send a messenger to you, your former training partner ..." He pointed to Squire Michael. "... but only if necessary."

Sir Theo nodded in understanding as they began to separate themselves and their teams from one another.

Sir Udo, the kingdom's captain of the guards, approached Duke Teufelmund. "What are your orders, Your Grace?"

Duke Teufelmund, starting to look a bit uneasy, replied, "Let us wait a few moments and allow the others to ride into their attack positions. We will then march straight and quiet until reaching the edge of the Saracen camp. When we see the red flag signals to our left and right, we will commence the charge."

The baron and Sir Theo, having split left and right, began moving separately but parallel to each other. Theo felt serious and determined as he led his team to the attack. He knew with certainty that the baron was mentally focused as well.

A short time passed. Duke Teufelmund and his men slowly began moving forward until the enemy camp came into sight. He raised a hand to signal a halt and looked left and right for the signals.

He thought he saw something red fluttering in the distance to his left. As he scanned right, another waving banner caught his eye. Neither flag was the intended signal ... they were actually Saracen tribal flags. The duke motioned to Sir Udo to join him as he continued to intensely scan either side of the camp.

"Do you see something?" asked Duke Teufelmund. "It looks to me like the signal banners but it is hard to be certain due to the distance. What say you?"

"I'm not sure, Your Grace," Sir Udo responded. "It doesn't look quite right to me."

The duke appeared exasperated and scanned left and right again. He saw the same fluttering as before, inhaled sharply through his nostrils, and made a fateful decision. "Those are the signal flags." He drew his sword and yelled, "Long live the king." He began his charge into the camp.

Sir Udo hesitated briefly before signaling the main force to follow. "Long live the king!" the men on horses shouted along with the foot soldiers who all sprinted toward the center of the camp.

As he rode into what at first looked like an empty camp, the duke heard a blood-chilling yell arise from the unsurprised Saracens. They rapidly began to spill out of their tents like giant ants and took the fight to the duke and his doomed men.

From a distance, Sir Theo heard the Saracen battle cries, but he was not yet in a position to attack. He was shocked and puzzled that the battle may have already begun. He continued forward more quickly with his men. Through the forest trees, they looked down in horror as they realized that Duke Teufelmund and his men had ridden into a slaughter. They were being attacked from all sides. A fierce fight ensued.

Why has the duke already started the battle? Theo asked himself. Then he saw the Saracen battle flags. They were blood red. He realized the duke must have mistaken them for the signal flags. He winced at what he was seeing and knew there was nothing he could do to change the outcome.

There was give and take with swords and arrows, but the main force was cut off and overwhelmed. Although they were on opposite sides of the battlefield and a distance from each other, Sir Theo caught a brief glimpse of the baron and his men. A moment later, looking again in the camp, he saw Duke Teufelmund pulled from his horse and surrounded by Saracens.

Theo peered again toward the baron who appeared to be motioning with his arm toward Squire Michael. Theo surmised the baron was telling the squire to seek out Sir Theo and his men so they could reassemble and determine the next course of action.

Squire Michael soon found Theo and his group and led them to the baron's location.

"A disaster," intoned Baron von Engel shaking his head as Theo approached.

Theo had rarely seen the baron look that dejected. "What of Duke Teufelmund and his men?" asked Sir Theo. "I could ascertain little from my vantage point once the duke was pulled from his horse."

"I sent Squire Thomas to look over the situation at the camp and see if any of our men have survived or escaped," replied the baron. "I expect him back soon. We must plan a new strategy as we wait for him to return."

Faruk stood with arms folded in the center of his tent. At his feet bound and gagged and lying face down was Duke Teufelmund and four of his men. The duke had identified himself moments earlier when they were dragged into the Saracen tent. All the kingdom soldiers, including the duke, were wounded to varying degrees. Two still had arrows sticking from their bodies.

Faruk looked toward Rami and Nijad. "Take them out and finish them. But leave this one here. I wish to speak to him before we send him to his God." Rami motioned to Nijad and the others to pick up and remove all the prisoners other than the duke.

The kingdom soldiers were roughly removed as Faruk stared silently at Duke Teufelmund. The Saracen leader was trying to take the measure of his prisoner. *Is he a brave soldier? A cold fish? Is he a true knight or something else?* Sounds of slashing blades and men groaning were heard while the duke dispassionately looked up at Faruk.

Faruk grabbed the duke's gag and forced him up from his stomach to his knees. He removed the gag and said, "Before you meet the same fate as your men, tell me what you hoped to achieve by being here."

"I could ask you the same," replied the duke calmly.

"As a courtesy to my noble prisoner, I will respond since the answer is simple. I wish not for this land but for wealth. And since I observed little reaction from you for the fate of your men, I suspect your motives are more complex than just protecting your king and your kingdom. Am I wrong? I can see that at least you are not a coward. Are you now showing me the face of a courageous noble resigned to his fate, or is it something else?"

"You are Faruk the Assassin?" asked Duke Teufelmund.

"I am."

"Then I have a proposal," said the duke. "I believe I know a way that will allow both of us to achieve our respective goals."

Theo looked up as Squire Thomas arrived by foot at their makeshift camp. He was helping to support a wounded Sir Udo. Two other soldiers limped together behind them. They approached the baron.

"What news?" the baron asked Sir Udo.

"Our men fought well. We must have killed forty or fifty of the marauders. But in the end, there were just too many of them. We were overwhelmed. The duke was pulled from his horse and wounded. He thought you had given your signal, but Squire Thomas explained that you had not done so nor were in position to attack. But I ... I managed to escape in the confusion of battle with these two men. We hid on the edge of the camp and watched as Duke Teufelmund and four others were taken alive and roughly dragged to the main tent, but ..." Sir Udo hesitated.

Sir Theo saw his grief and grabbed Sir Udo's arm. "Go on, Sir Knight."

Sir Udo turned away from Sir Theo, looked around at the rest of the group, and continued with his eyes cast to the ground. "Our men were taken out of the tent and butchered ... butchered without any warning or ceremony!"

"What of Duke Teufelmund?" asked Baron von Engel.

"I never saw him come out of the tent," Sir Udo said.

"Ransom?" Sir Theo asked as he turned toward the baron.

"Little doubt," responded the baron. He asked Sir Udo, "How many fighters would you say Faruk has left?"

"Hard to be certain, Your Grace, but I would estimate no more than two dozen," replied Sir Udo.

"I would agree with that number from what I could see," Squire Thomas said.

"And the tent with Faruk and Duke Teufelmund is at the south end of the camp?" asked the baron.

"Yes," Sir Udo responded. "It's the largest one. There's no mistaking it."

"Very well," the baron said. "We must try to rescue the duke. A new attack is needed from the east and west but with some sort of a diversion from the north. It will be a variation of our original plan. We must move quickly and this time ensure surprise. I don't think they are expecting us to counterattack now."

The baron bent over and started drawing a plan in the ground as Sir Theo, Sir Udo, and the others watched intently.

The duke sat unceremoniously in a corner of Faruk's tent. He had been unbound and was having his wounds treated by a Saracen healer. Faruk huddled with Rami and Nijad over a table in the center. It was growing dark when the three men simultaneously heard shouting and saw a red glow through the tent. Faruk motioned to the duke and his caregiver to stay. He and the others raced outside. They saw multiple fires at the north end of the camp.

"Infidels!" shouted Faruk. "Bows and swords!"

The kingdom soldiers raced into the camp from the east and west with a great yell. Hand-to-hand fighting ensued; it was clear that the Saracens had been caught off guard.

Faruk ran back to his tent. He entered and found his healer groaning on the ground and rubbing his head. The duke was nowhere to be seen. Faruk snorted as he seized his dagger and scimitar and ran outside. Rami and Nijad raced up to him.

"The fight is lost, Faruk. We were surprised," Rami said through clenched teeth.

Faruk saw Baron von Engel looking toward him with a group of men. Faruk's eyes opened wide, and his nostrils flared. "All is not lost. We will have our revenge. And more important, we will still have our reward. Quickly follow me to the south. I will explain once we are safe."

The last of the Saracens in the camp continued to fight the baron and his men, but they proved to be no match for the kingdom warriors and were quickly dispatched. The enemy was soundly defeated. The kingdom men rallied. They all were now battle-tested soldiers.

Sir Theo, with Duke Teufelmund's arm over his shoulder, suddenly appeared from near the tent and approached the group. The baron saw them and smiled.

"What of Faruk?" asked Sir Theo.

"Heading south with a few of his men ... and in rather a big hurry," replied the baron with a sly smile.

He then looked at the duke. "And you, Your Grace? How goes it?"

"It goes," responded the tired and wounded duke.

Baron von Engel nodded to the duke, winked at Sir Theo, and turned to his victorious men. "Long live the king!"

"Long live the king!" they shouted in response as the duke bowed his head and said nothing.

"Squire Michael," the baron called out.

"Your Grace," Squire Michael answered.

"Take our fastest horse and ride back to the kingdom. Inform King Johann what has transpired here. Tell him we have suffered losses but our men fought bravely and we have won the day."

Squire Michael bowed. "Yes, Your Grace."

A guard on the castle wall squinted as he saw a rider coming. He recognized him and shouted to the guards below, "Open the gate and alert the king. Squire Michael approaches."

The gate began to open. After being informed of the new arrival, King Johann raced to the courtyard. He and Squire Michael arrived almost simultaneously.

"What news?" asked the anxious king as the squire dismounted and ran to his monarch.

"Good news, Majesty" replied Michael almost breathlessly. "We suffered losses, but in the end, we won the day. Duke Teufelmund was wounded and captured by the enemy, but he was rescued by Sir Theo."

The king smiled broadly.

"The initial main force attack led by the duke failed, but our men fought valiantly against the Saracens. Baron von Engel devised a different fight plan with a new diversion that proved successful."

"And what of Faruk?" asked the king.

"Escaped, Highness. Gone into hiding along with a few of his men. The baron and Sir Theo stayed behind along with the able bodied to dispose of our dead. They thought it best to have Duke Teufelmund and our wounded return as soon as possible. The baron commanded that I ride ahead with all due speed to deliver the news of our victory."

"Good," noted the king. "Good. You have done well."

The king then turned toward the main gate. "Guards! Prepare to receive our wounded and the remainder of the king's guard when they return."

He turned back to the castle and saw Bishop Kohlhaas approaching the courtyard. "Eminence! I need a private word with you."

The bishop bowed and walked to the king.

The sun began to set after another long day. The baron, Sir Theo, and the remainder of the kingdom force stopped at the edge of the forest near the lake.

A short distance away hidden in the trees, Faruk the Assassin watched the return home of the kingdom's forces. Rami and Nijad knelt close to him. Faruk's head silently bobbed up and down with the satisfaction and knowledge of what was to come.

Theo and the baron paused briefly and drank in the magnificent and welcome sight of the castle off in the distance. They slapped each other's shoulders. They acknowledged the foot soldiers with fist salutes. The lead party encouraged their horses forward.

When the column of victors entered the castle a brief time later, they experienced great fanfare. The king and queen led the cheers and promised a celebration the next day. Theo learned from Squire Michael that Duke Teufelmund and the other wounded soldiers had arrived earlier and were being cared for in the infirmary.

Princess Margarethe approached Baron von Engel and Theo. She congratulated the baron on his success. She then turned to Theo and wordlessly looked at him in a way he had never experienced. There had always been a special connection between them but nothing quite like that. Theo felt completed and uplifted as never before. If there had ever been an emptiness in his soul, she had just filled it.

Sir Theo and the baron were quickly surrounded by many others from the castle. The princess departed with the royal party to prepare for the fest.

Theo acknowledged and appreciated the adulation thrust upon him, but he was exhausted by all that had occurred over the past few days. He had been tested in battle and was satisfied that he had met the challenge. But his body ached. He looked after his men and his horse before seeking out his room and collapsing in bed.

Before he drifted to sleep, his thoughts were of the princess and what would become of them. As the arms of Morpheus began to seize him, he was distressed and troubled by the uncertain future. Theo's slumber was deep but troubled. He dreamed he saw Faruk aiming his crossbow at a shadow. Theo began to sweat profusely as the shadow came into focus. It was Princess Margarethe.

He abruptly awoke and sat up in bed, startled and breathing heavily. He started to breathe more easily when he realized he had been dreaming. However, he felt something was wrong and was worried as never before.

As promised, there was a large fest and celebration the next day. Off in a corner of the great hall, Queen Annemarie and Baron von Engel observed Princess Margarethe and Sir Theo, who seemed to have eyes only for each other. The queen looked at them with a private sadness. She knew that their future together could not be as husband and wife.

The queen noticed the king stand, and the noisy hall quickly became silent. He scanned the room and began to address his subjects. "I speak tonight with great joy and gratitude. Our military and its leaders have served the kingdom well. I have met with my advisors and wish to make several royal announcements. But this can wait till the morrow. Tonight, we celebrate!" he said as he lifted his cup.

Cheers of "Long live the king!" erupted. The king smiled and held out his goblet to all. The queen turned her attention back to Princess Margarethe and Sir Theo. She was pleased they were caught up in the moment of celebration, but then she became sad as they returned to gazing at one other.

Queen Annemarie stood and smiled regally at her husband. She glanced once more at the princess and Theo. She turned to Baron von Engel. "May I have a private word, Your Grace?"

"Of course, Highness," he responded. "May I ask of what you wish to speak?"

"Two subjects, my dear Baron. Triumph and tragedy," replied the queen with a sigh.

The following day, a great crowd gathered in the castle courtyard for the king's special announcements. Theo saw the monarch approaching and motioned to Squire Michael. The squire leaned over the balcony and called out, "The king!"

The king appeared on the balcony and looked over all those assembled in the courtyard. Someone shouted, "Long live the king," and the entire crowd in one voice took up the chant. King Johann spread his arms, smiled, and quieted them.

"I have three important announcements I wish to make. For the first, I call forward Sir Theo."

Sir Theo was caught a bit off guard, but he quickly recovered himself, walked briskly to the king, and bowed.

King Johann continued. "One of the welcome responsibilities and pleasures of being king is to recognize and reward great deeds performed by our subjects. I give you Sir Theo, who as a child and now as a grown man has served this kingdom with distinction and profound results. His family has a tradition of bravery that he has further enhanced."

The king motioned to Baron von Engel, who carried a magnificent sword to him. "This sword took Sir Ducu, our master-at-arms, many years to make. It was designed and forged with the certainty that this day would come." The king partially drew the sword. "Your parents may not be here, but their names are immortalized on the blade ... Sir Josef and Lady Lorraine."

The king sheathed the blade and handed it to Sir Theo, who took it with both hands. Theo instinctively kissed the scabbard and then pressed it to his heart.

The king continued. "His great deeds stretch across many years ... from his childhood bravery to just a few days ago, which included mortal battle and daring rescue. So for now and henceforth, I proclaim him Graf Theo, Count of Tyrol and Lord of Tyrol Castle. He is now and will remain a member of this royal court and is welcomed into the kingdom's family of nobility."

The crowd cheered as Count Theo struggled to control his emotions. Baron von Engel clapped him on the back. Theo noticed that Princess Margarethe was beaming. The queen forced a smile as the baron led Count Theo a few steps away. It seemed strange to Theo that the baron began to wear a serious expression.

The king, still smiling, turned back to the crowd and motioned for silence. "The second announcement is brief but significant. After long consultations with my advisors, I wish to address the kingdom's succession of rule. When the time comes, it is my royal decree that Princess Margarethe will succeed me on the kingdom throne."

Cheers rang out followed by enthusiastic applause. A somewhat surprised but regal princess looked to her father and bowed to him and then the crowd. She reached out, found Queen Annemarie's and Lady Marianne's hands, and squeezed them tightly.

"And finally," said the king, "I have a very welcome announcement involving Duke Teufelmund and the future of our kingdom. The duke has recently approached me and requested the hand of Princess Margarethe in marriage ... and I have pledged to him my approval."

The crowd began to politely applaud. The queen looked to Princess Margarethe as did Theo. The princess had turned ashen. The queen propped up her daughter the best she could; the princess was struggling to stand.

As he stood on the end of the balcony away from the royal family, Theo suddenly felt the baron grab his arm. Theo was desperate and stunned. He opened his mouth to say something but not before Baron von Engel quickly turned to face him. The baron took his other arm and, as he held both, discretely shook his head. The baron's eyes widened and it was clear he intended the newly anointed Count of Tyrol to be silent.

Theo, after years of practice taking cues from his mentor and surrogate father, pursed his lips. He whispered to the baron, "It is my greatest day ... It is my worst day."

"Theo ... Your Grace," the baron said. "You are now a member of the nobility. You must always act the part especially in difficult times."

As he looked up past the baron toward the princess, Theo saw a tear streaming down her cheek as she looked back at him.

King Johann realized his final decree had not been received as he had expected. But he was the king and had made his decision. "These royal decrees are my commands and are to be respected and obeyed."

Suddenly, Theo heard the familiar whoosh of an arrow and saw it strike the king squarely in the chest. Then, as he turned with pain and surprise on his face, another struck King Johann in the back. The queen rushed to him shouting "Johann!" and she too was struck twice with arrows and collapsed. Count Theo saw sudden panic all around as he shouted, "Protect the princess!"

Guards rushed onto the balcony as Duke Teufelmund ran inside to safety. Squire Michael pointed to the castle wall and shouted, "Up there! There! Two assassins!"

Theo and the baron looked at each other and exclaimed, "Faruk!"

The Saracen brothers, Rami and Nijad, deftly escaped over the wall with the help of a rope being held at the bottom by Faruk to aid in their escape. Guards ran in all directions.

Princess Margarethe, surrounded by guards, was sobbing and shaking as she stared at her motionless parents. Lady Marianne tried her best to comfort the princess as they were led to safety by the guards.

The baron leaned over the bodies. He stood and said, "The king is dead." He looked toward the departing princess. "Long live the queen."

"How did Faruk gain access to the castle so easily? There's more to this than meets the eye," Count Theo said.

"Aye," responded the baron. "It is a cruel, hard thing. But we must learn all that we can. I will immediately request a meeting of the privy council and pray for God's help and for our new queen. Now that you are a noble, you must join us as we discuss the day's events and make the necessary plans."

Faruk and his accomplices, after a hard ride, reached the edge of the kingdom woods.

"You have your revenge," said Rami as Nijad nodded.

"We have more than that, my friends," said Faruk. "And there is even more to come. Revenge may be sweet, but I'm not yet done with this kingdom and its wealth. The king may be dead, but a new queen still lives. We will soon collect our promised reward and return home. In time, we will likely be welcomed back for more work."

With a slight smile, a determined-looking Faruk pulled his horse's reins and galloped off deep into the forest. The brothers followed.

7

Innsbruck, Austria
Present Day

Cubby and Carmen sat silently with their mouths open. Otto looked back and forth at them and sensed their distress. "I'm afraid I have upset you more than I intended. Perhaps we should stop," he said.

"It's so, so sad," said Carmen to no one in particular. "I can't believe things like that can really happen."

"This is even more intense than my video games!" Cubby said prompting Carmen to roll her eyes. The tension started to ease.

Otto reached toward a pocket in his vest as he felt his phone vibrate. He took it out and looked at the screen. It was Friederun, the children's mother, calling. "Hello." He paused to listen. "Yes ma'am. Cubby and Carmen are here with me." Otto held out his phone. "Say hello to your mother."

"Hey, Mom!" they said.

"Yes," Otto responded after he returned the phone to his ear and continued the call. "No problem whatsoever. We are in the middle of our story and are still in the Silver Chapel. Take your time. I'll call if we finish before you return. Good. Tschüss!"

"What did Mom say?" asked Carmen.

"Your mother said that your father was delayed at work and had just arrived for lunch," replied Otto. "She wanted to know if it was okay if she returned a bit later than expected."

"No problem," said Cubby. "That means you can finish the story. But what was that word you just used before hanging up with Mom?"

"You mean 'Tschüss?'" Otto asked.

"Yes, that's the one," Carmen said. "I wondered about that myself."

"A fair question," Otto said. "It sort of sounds like combining the English words *choose* and *juice*. It's similar to when you say 'Bye' in English or 'Ciao' in Italian. We normally use it with family and friends here in Austria or Germany when we part with one another. Tschüss!" he repeated as he waved good-bye to an imaginary person. "Now shall I continue? There's still more to tell."

"Highs and lows?" asked Carmen.

"Highs ... and lows," responded Otto.

8

The Kingdom Castle AD 1120

As the king and queen's bodies lay in state next to the main altar of the kingdom chapel, the privy council met in the throne room. Previously, the council was composed of only three members: Duke Teufelmund, Baron von Engel, and Bishop Kohlhaas. Following his elevation to nobility, Count Theo joined the council as a fourth.

He tried to keep his emotions in check but found that difficult. With all that had happened—the battle, the announcement that the princess would marry the duke despite Theo's elevation to nobility, the assassinations of the king and queen at the hands of Faruk—it was almost too much for him to bear. Theo told himself to be brave, but he felt defeated.

The voices of the other three council members blended. Theo fought with himself to focus. But just then, the soon-to-be queen entered the room. He wanted nothing more than to hold and comfort her, but his heart sank even deeper knowing such an embrace would never be possible.

Princess Margarethe had Lady Marianne at her side as she walked toward the throne. The princess was dressed in a mix of black and white with a black headpiece. The men became silent and stood. The princess, her face drawn and eyes rubbed red, walked to the throne. She touched the throne's arm gently as if it were her father's hand. She then turned and sat.

Bishop Kohlhaas spoke first. "As heir apparent, Your Highness needs to rest and pray for strength."

"I am resting," she responded. "And I have been in the chapel praying over the king and queen. The kingdom and its people are my strength. All of you, as the privy council, are my advisors. I am here now for your advice and good counsel." She adjusted herself more comfortably on the throne and acted resigned to the tragedy. "Now, what can you tell me of the recent ... events?"

Duke Teufelmund spoke. "Highness, the final arrangements for your parents' internment in the chapel are underway. They should be completed by late tomorrow. And with our deepest sympathy to you in these circumstances, your coronation ceremony should take place as soon as possible. I hesitate to mention it, but there is the matter of the king's wish for our ... the marriage. A date must soon be set."

"And what of those who murdered the king and queen?" the princess asked ignoring the issues raised by the duke.

"We sent soldiers to the woods but lost their trail," replied the baron. "I regret to report they have escaped."

"And who are these men?"

The baron continued. "We believe there are three Saracen culprits—Faruk the assassin and two of his men."

"They are all assassins," the princess said. "How did they manage to access the castle so easily?"

"That we do not yet know, Highness," responded the baron.

"We have not yet heard from the Count of Tyrol," stated the princess as she looked at Theo without emotion. "What say you, Your Grace?"

"Your Highness," he responded with a bow, "I share your deep sorrow and understand your grief. Please know that I, we, will serve you and the kingdom as we served the king. Your wishes and desires in the matters now before us, as well as those yet to come, will be supported by all here assembled."

"Very well. I welcome such support," the princess said. She addressed the bishop. "Eminence, the funeral mass will take place in two days."

"Yes, Your Highness," replied the bishop. "And the coronation and wedding?"

"Ah, yes. The coronation and wedding. Our customary period of mourning is two weeks, so my coronation and wedding will take place a fortnight after the funeral. Can we perform both ceremonies together?"

After a brief hesitation, the bishop responded, "Yes, Highness. It is not usual to combine such auspicious events, but given the circumstances, I see no problem if that is your wish."

"So then it shall be," replied Princess Margarethe as she looked at those assembled and glanced at Lady Marianne. "I have much to mourn, but more important, we have much to do for our kingdom."

The princess stood regally and proceeded from the room followed by Lady Marianne. All the men present bowed in respect. They straightened up as she exited. Bishop Kohlhaas spoke. "The great shadow over us begins to lift." He clasped his hands as if to pray. "All praise to God's goodness and mercy. We have ourselves ... a queen!"

Lady Marianne knew well what it was like to suffer loss but not to the same extent as did Princess Margarethe. They trusted each other without question. As the fortnight mourning period drew to a close and after much sharing of each other's thoughts, their private discussions led to a few significant decisions. The plans they made together in private would greatly impact their lives and destinies.

As they sat and earnestly talked in the princess's room, the sun was preparing to set. The next day, after all the coronation and wedding ceremonies, Margarethe would move to the royal chambers along with her new husband, Duke Teufelmund. But for the time being, they discussed only each other and Count Theo.

Lady Marianne spoke. "You have suffered much." She took the princess's hands in hers. "It gives me great joy and solace to help bring you some measure of happiness before your big day tomorrow."

"Then it's decided. Marianne, there is no dearer friend in the world than you." They hugged. "Your advice and support mean everything to me and have greatly eased my pain."

"All right then," continued the princess as she sat upright and looked at her best friend. "Let us begin since the time grows late." They reached out, held each other's arms, and hugged again. The princess sat back and smiled as Marianne stood and departed the bedchamber.

As she briskly walked through the castle to the courtyard, Marianne smiled as she considered the events about to unfold. She did not know if the plans she and her best friend made would take place as hoped, but there was no question they were worth trying. It was time to find Count Theo.

After exiting the castle, Lady Marianne promptly found him in the courtyard. His head was hanging down and he was moving it solemnly from side to side. Theo was being consoled by Baron von Engel, whose hand rested on his shoulder.

"Your Grace," Marianne said with a bow, "Princess Margarethe requests an audience. I am to take you to her."

"Now?" asked Theo.

Marianne smiled and nodded.

Theo looked at the baron quizzically. The baron pushed him to his feet. "Go now. Go, my son. And do the bidding of our princess who on the morrow will be our queen!"

Still a bit confused, Theo looked at Marianne and motioned for her to lead on. The baron smiled and winked at Marianne, who noted his reaction but did not respond.

As they walked, Theo opened his heart to Marianne. "It is painful for me to see the princess on the eve of this wedding. You know how I feel about her."

Marianne stopped in her tracks and looked Theo in the eye. "We are lifelong friends, you and I and Margarethe. I tell you in deep confidence that our beloved princess feels the same about you. But she is to be the queen and has no choice but to honor her father's decree. You both must be brave no matter how bitter the circumstances."

Theo slowly nodded and replied. "Marianne, you are a trusted friend to us both. I am deeply grateful that you are part of our lives."

Marianne smiled in approval and understanding. The plan was starting to work. She quickly and discreetly led Theo through the castle to the room where the princess awaited. He realized he had never been in that part of the castle before even as a child. After walking up several staircases, Marianne turned down a hallway, stopped, and knocked on a door.

"Come in," responded the princess as she bid him enter.

The door opened. Theo stooped down and began to enter with

hesitation and, as he saw the princess, immediately straightened up and managed to hit his head squarely on the doorframe. He grabbed the top of his head and then steadied himself. Princess Margarethe, for the first time in some weeks, laughed out loud and then covered her mouth with her hand. Theo signaled silently that he was fine.

Lady Marianne looked at the princess, rolled her eyes, smiled, and exited the bedchamber while closing the door behind her. She moved a chair in the hallway closer to the doorway. She then sat, crossed her arms, and smiled knowingly to herself as she began to stand guard.

It was one of the few times Margarethe and Theo had been alone together. After an awkward silence, she spoke.

"Count Theo," Margarethe began, "are you all right?"

"Yes, Highness," responded Theo somewhat embarrassed. He then straightened up and looked serious. "How may I serve you?"

"As you know, I will wed tomorrow," she stated matter-of-factly and looked down. She raised her head and gazed at Theo with great warmth. "I have two special favors to ask of you."

Theo bowed.

Margarethe continued. "First, I wish for you to marry soon and strive to find happiness with another."

Theo paused. "May I speak freely, Your Highness?" After she nodded, he continued. "I've always wished to live my life with you and only you. Besides, who else would have me?"

"Theo, I'm sure many women would. But I ask that you consider Lady Marianne. She is a dear friend and confidant to us both. I know absolutely that she would agree with this proposal."

"But ... I ... I love only you," replied Theo. "That's the truth of it."

"And I you," responded Margarethe as she touched his arm. "But circumstances have thrust this hard duty on us. If I knew you would consider Marianne, that would be a great comfort to me. You would be paired with a good woman."

Theo was silent for a moment. "What is the other favor you request?"

Margarethe looked at him and confessed, "I must ask you something neither as a princess nor someone not yet a queen."

Theo looked at her questioningly.

She continued. "I ask that you and I spend this night ... together."

Theo flinched. Obviously in a profound state of dilemma, he stammered, "Highness! Your position ... me ... I'm not ..."

She put two fingers on his lips. "Theo," she stated with all the love in her heart, "I have given this much thought, and I know you are conflicted between love and honor. But this is also very much my love, my honor. I hoped always for my lips to be touched by yours before any others. I have thought about this long and hard. If I must begin to be the kingdom queen tomorrow and for the rest of my life, I desire for us to have at least this one night to try to ease our pain ... if only for a brief moment. I wish here and now to be nothing more than Margarethe, who loves you with all her being. It is the only gift my true heart can give to you before tomorrow." Her eyes filled with tears. "If you love me more than yourself, you will grant this one—"

Theo abruptly seized her head and kissed her forehead, looked her in the eyes, and kissed her properly. He pulled back and simply said, "My ... sweet ... heart." He kissed her again as her arms encircled his body.

The sun set as they embraced and continued to kiss with abandon.

As the morning light began to peek over the horizon, Theo finished dressing. He smiled at Margarethe. He thought she was still sleeping, but she was actually awake and looking at him through her partially opened eyelashes. He took a few steps toward her and stroked her face gently. She fully opened her eyes, looked at Theo, and beamed a face full of love.

"I must go," he said.

"I know." She reached under the bed and handed Theo a small item. "But take this with you."

Theo looked and realized it was the pouch he used to wear around his neck that contained the infinity sign. He opened it, looked inside, smiled, and pressed the hand holding it to his heart. He then exited the bedchamber with a final backward glance and again managed to hit his head on the doorway. Margarethe cupped her mouth with both hands to stifle a laugh. Theo rubbed his head and then shook it in disbelief. They exchanged a final smile that was stamped forever in each other's mind and heart.

Before the door was closed, Margarethe could see a still alert Lady Marianne looking up to Theo from her chair. He removed his right hand from his head, grabbed Marianne's hand, squeezed it, and then raised it to his lips to kiss. They wordlessly stared at each other before Theo turned, gently closed the door, and departed.

Margarethe lay back on her bed for a final, brief moment of serenity before the day's demanding ceremonies ... and slowly smiled her greatest-ever smile.

Several hours later amid appropriate pomp and circumstance, Margarethe was crowned the kingdom queen by Bishop Kohlhaas. He then married her and Duke Teufelmund.

Count Theo and Lady Marianne spent much of the day together discussing the future. That night while in the receiving line at the wedding reception, they announced to Queen Margarethe and Duke Teufelmund their intention to marry. The queen and her new husband, now a royal consort, appeared greatly pleased and gave Theo and Marianne their blessing.

When she and Count Theo married a few months after the coronation, Lady Marianne became Countess Marianne of Tyrol. They took up residence at the count's new estate, Castle Tyrol, not far from the kingdom castle.

Somewhat less than a year after the coronation, Queen Margarethe gave birth to twins, Princess Victoria and Princess Allison. Several months after that, Count Theo and Countess Marianne also welcomed twin girls, Lady Cristina and Lady Stephanie.

The many years that passed proved to be among the most peaceful and productive ever experienced in the kingdom.

9

THE KINGDOM LAKE AD 1130

Queen Margarethe and Countess Marianne looked on as four young girls played by the lake near the castle. The blond maidens held hands and circled around in a ring with laughter and smiles. Their mothers watched from a short distance away. The queen considered the scene to be idyllic. They were prospering as was the kingdom under the queen's rule. But equally important to her was that all the girls had a reputation of having good hearts. It was a welcome comment both mothers often heard as they moved about in the kingdom.

Marianne smiled, turned from the children toward Margarethe, and said, "We have much to be grateful for with our girls and the peace in the kingdom."

"Yes we do. But I fear the duke grows tired of me," the queen casually commented. Marianne was silent. "And how is Theo?" asked Margarethe trying to change the subject.

Marianne wanted to respond to her first comment but decided it was better to simply answer her question. She grasped the queen's hand. "You know Theo. He is such a good man, and he looks after us all. He is dedicated to his duties and responsibilities with family and the kingdom."

"I certainly know that he and Duke Teufelmund do not agree on many of the issues involving the kingdom," said the queen.

"But we also know that the bishop and the baron sometimes disagree as well. It is the way of such men," the countess said.

The queen nodded and concurred. "It is so. We must let them debate until they believe they have won ... or at least convince themselves they have."

The queen and the countess gave each other knowing looks, smiled, and turned back to the girls at play.

Men argued and shouted in the great hall. Bishop Kohlhaas banged his crosier on the floor to bring all to order. "Each of us is troubled with this news of a possible threat to the kingdom. Calm and organized discussion must take place so we can inform the queen and suggest to her a plan on how best to handle the situation. Let us review the facts. It appears that Henry the Proud, Duke of Bavaria, is encamped with a large army in the kingdom forest about two days' ride from here. His intentions are unknown."

The baron stared at the bishop with raised eyebrows and a look of uncertainty.

"Then we must immediately ride out and present a show of force," Duke Teufelmund said.

"Your grace, please hear me out," responded Count Theo. "A small probing force would be the wiser initial action. Henry the Proud reportedly has an army far superior to anything we could muster. We must first determine the extent of the threat. If he is simply moving through the kingdom, there is no cause for concern. But if he means us harm, Queen Margarethe and the kingdom must be protected with the bulk of our forces here at the castle."

"I strongly agree," exclaimed the baron. He looked around the room searching for others who felt the same.

Bishop Kohlhaas scanned the great hall as well for consensus with Theo's proposal. "Who among you concurs with first using a small probing force?" he asked.

Shouts of "Aye" and "Yea" filled the hall in addition to numerous heads nodding in agreement.

"Very well," stated the bishop firmly. "I will advise the queen both of the situation and our proposed initial action to send out a small force in an effort to determine Henry the Proud's intentions. I will ask Count Theo and Baron von Engel to lead this small group subject to final approval by the queen."

The count and baron nodded in agreement as Duke Teufelmund, looking unhappy, abruptly turned and exited the great hall. The duke went to the royal bedchamber shaking his head and looking much like a man who had lost one too many battles. He heard a noise and was startled when a hooded figure stepped from behind the window curtain. The duke drew a dagger. "Show yourself and state your business!"

The figure slowly pulled back his hood. It was Faruk the Assassin.

"I am here to complete my pact with you ... the one we agreed upon when you were my prisoner those many years ago. You do remember our discussion?" asked Faruk.

"Of course I do. And I also remember that I paid you well for sparing my life and for taking the first step to secure the kingdom throne for myself."

"Ah, yes," replied Faruk. "Thanks to you, I became wealthy and have since been known to my people as Faruk the Royal Assassin. But time has moved on. I am again in need of gold, and it appears you are still in need of becoming king. I thought perhaps the queen might be gone by now through some ... accident or such? But I understand that she still lives."

"Much has happened over the past ten years," responded the duke. "I have children although my heirs are ... female. Other than that unfortunate fact, I no longer have a need for a wife or a queen. Plus, there is now a new threat to consider. Henry the Proud and his army are currently encamped in the kingdom forest. But you may once again prove to be useful to me." Teufelmund paused. "And I'm sure more gold would be of use to you?"

Faruk smiled in obvious agreement. He had learned to put a value on certain wealth as opposed to potential risk. Besides, the future was closer to him at that point than it had been ten years earlier, and he had to prepare for it. He was only in the middle of his life, but hard living was beginning to take its toll.

"Good, then," stated the duke. "We again have a way to resolve your need for gold and provide me the opportunity to secure the throne."

Queen Margarethe and Bishop Kohlhaas met privately in the throne room. She sat with her fingers intertwined and her hands close to her chin as she listened to the bishop.

"... So that is what we recommend, Your Majesty. This potential threat to us concerning Henry the Proud cannot be ignored. Count Theo and Baron von Engel will ride out early tomorrow with just a few men. They will confirm the strength of the army and, if possible, determine Henry the Proud's intentions."

"Very well," responded the queen. "But we must prepare and remain on constant vigil for any and all enemies far or near. The kingdom must not suffer as it has in the past."

"I thank Your Highness for your approval and will ask the count and the baron to prepare themselves and their men."

The bishop bowed and departed the room. Queen Margarethe sat on the throne looking pensive and concerned. Four young girls trailed by Countess Marianne burst in and ran to her for hugs. She embraced them all lovingly and looked at Marianne. "You and the girls must stay at the castle for now. It will be safer until we learn more about Henry the Proud and his intentions toward the kingdom." The queen looked again at the girls and hugged them tighter. She stared at the ceiling unsure of the future.

The following morning, Count Theo and Baron von Engel rode out of the castle with six knights as the queen looked on. Countess Marianne and the four girls, sleepy and still in their nightclothes, stood next to the queen and waved from the castle as the perilous adventure began.

Once the advance party moved out of sight, Margarethe sighed with worry but then turned and spoke to the girls. "Shall we meet for lunch in the garden?" she asked. Marianne smiled in agreement.

The queen saw the duke observing the morning's proceedings from one of the upper castle towers. She could not be sure, but she thought he was grinning ... something she rarely saw him do. When he saw the queen looking at him, his expression darkened as he slightly bowed toward her.

Faruk met with Rami and Nijad on the edge of the forest. He explained that he met with Duke Teufelmund and had been given a special mission. It was for more gold than they could have ever expected. They must only eliminate a woman in the castle.

"Today is the day. It will be a fast in and out as before," said Faruk. "I will help with the escape."

"How will we know the woman?" asked Rami.

"She is fair and will likely be with two girls who are not to be harmed. You and Nijad will scale the castle wall as before. Unless you are too old now?"

Rami and Nijad scowled. Faruk smiled as he gave each a piece of gold. "Here is something to help you climb that rope ... and there will be much more awaiting for us all when our work is completed."

They looked at each other approvingly.

"Now let us plan our task," Faruk said.

Count Theo and Baron von Engel rode at the front of their small group. Theo was silent, but the baron suddenly began to reminisce about his war experiences. He spoke of his first meeting in Jerusalem with Queen Margarethe's father, King Johann, and their many adventures together. The baron, who was in an atypically open mood, also waxed nostalgic about his family and his former estate being destroyed while he was away fighting in the crusade.

"Were the cowards ever brought to heel?" inquired Theo.

"Oh yes," replied the baron. He paused briefly to relish the justice contained in his brief response. "Afterward, King Johann invited me to join his kingdom, which is where I've found a soldier's peace and a good life."

"What know you of Henry the Proud, Duke of Bavaria?" asked Theo.

"First of all, he is a proud man," answered the baron with a smile. "But I know him, Theo, and I am not convinced he wishes any harm for the kingdom."

"How can you be sure?"

"I cannot. But my instincts tell me that we are up against some sort of threat. If not Henry the Proud, then it's someone else."

It was almost noon at the kingdom castle. The queen and her daughters were spending time with the kitchen staff and enjoying an informal chat and a tasting with Ingeborg, the royal cook.

Countess Marianne was still in the main castle helping dress her girls before lunch. She finished brushing Lady Cristina's and Lady Stephanie's hair. The three entered the castle hallway on their way to the garden.

The queen, still in the kitchen, tasted the luncheon soup. She smiled at Ingeborg and approved the soup with her eyes. She gave Princess Victoria and Princess Allison a taste as well, which quickly prompted them to ask for another spoonful.

The team of three Saracens moved with stealth toward the castle and began climbing a rampart leading to a battlement. Faruk aimed his crossbow and shot a shaft with an attached grappling hook over the top of the castle wall. He pulled the rope taut and signaled the brothers to begin their climb. He waited at the bottom as he had done years earlier. Rami and Nijad silently climbed the battlement overlooking the garden and took positions just inside the garden wall. Rami scanned the area for their target as Nijad looked out for guards. All was quiet. They patiently lay in wait for their opportunity. Rami looked at Nijad, who wore something of a smirk in anticipation of their success and ultimate reward.

Directly under them but unseen by either brother, the queen stepped outside the kitchen with her daughters. She stopped a few steps from the kitchen doorway and smiled as she saw Countess Marianne, Lady Cristina, and Lady Stephanie approaching from the opposite end of the garden. She waved a greeting along with Princess Victoria and Princess Allison, who were standing next to her.

The countess continued walking and waved back as did her girls. The quiet was suddenly broken by a whistling arrow. It struck a still-smiling Marianne squarely in the chest. She gasped and crumpled to the ground. Her girls knelt next to her and cried, "Mutti, Mutti!" They shook their mother vigorously as if to wake her.

A shocked Queen Margarethe grasped her own chest and silently mouthed the word "Marianne!" She screamed "Guards! Guards!"

As Rami and Nijad began their escape toward the battlement, the queen pushed her girls back toward Ingeborg in the kitchen. "Stay here and watch them!"

Margarethe raced to Marianne as guards swarmed the garden. She heard one shout "The garden battlement!" as he pointed at the Saracens climbing over the castle wall.

The queen reached Marianne, who was alive but fading rapidly.

The girls, shocked and frightened, still clung to their mother and were crying. A guard approached, and the queen quickly commanded him, "Take the girls to Ingeborg in the kitchen!" She then lifted and cradled Marianne in her arms and said, "The girls will be safe. Help is on the way."

Through her pain and tears, Marianne spoke haltingly. "Margarethe ... please care for the girls as if they were your own." The queen nodded and began to cry. "Do what you can to look after Theo." The queen nodded again. "Tell him I thank him for being my hero. I love you with all my heart," were Marianne's last words as her head dropped over to one side.

The queen wailed. It was a sound anyone who heard would never forget. It echoed throughout the castle. She clutched Marianne, rocked her, and sobbed uncontrollably.

Guards continued pouring onto the battlement and could see the two assassins going down a rope while a third awaited them at the bottom. In a moment, the three sped off to their horses and mounted quickly. A guard with a crossbow took careful aim and struck the tallest of the Saracens in the neck. Nijad was dead before his body hit the ground. Seconds later, several guards on horseback chased after the surviving Saracens while a few guards on foot stopped next to the body of Nijad. They announced loudly that he was dead.

Duke Teufelmund appeared at the top of the battlement and yelled "Treachery! Treachery by the hand of Henry the Proud! The queen has been assassinated!"

"Milord," shouted a guard climbing up from the garden area. "It was Countess Marianne who was struck down. The queen lives!"

Duke Teufelmund was perplexed. He looked over the castle grounds. He quietly whispered, "Long live the queen."

A short time later, Bishop Kohlhaas rode past the lake up to the edge of the forest with several guards. He stopped, dismounted, and saw Sir Michael, who years earlier had been Squire Michael the messenger.

"What news, Sir Michael?" asked the bishop.

"Eminence, we caught the remaining two assassins just as they reached the forest," responded Sir Michael. "One is dead and the other wounded but very much alive."

"Take me to him," said the bishop.

They found Faruk tied to a tree with an arrow sticking from his thigh. Bishop Kohlhaas motioned to Sir Michael for privacy as Faruk struggled against his bonds.

"And who might you be?" asked the bishop.

"I am Faruk ... Faruk, the Royal Assassin," he proudly stated.

"Well Faruk, methinks you may soon join your victims in death," the bishop said. "The only question is if it will be a slow, painful experience or mercifully fast."

"You are a man of the cloth?" asked Faruk. Bishop Kohlhaas nodded. "How can you speak to me in such a way?"

The bishop bent over him and casually removed his gloves. "I was a chaplain in the crusade. I know your Saracen ways. I also know that many of my military brothers met their fate mercifully on the battlefield and unmercifully as prisoners. You were here to make mischief, and you did us great harm today. Tell me what you know and I can promise you a swift death."

Faruk responded coolly. "If I must confess my sins to a Christian, I need a promise of life, not death."

"Why should I spare you after what you and your fellow Saracens have done?"

"Because I can tell you more than you think I know or can even think to ask."

"Such as?" Bishop Kohlhaas responded with casual interest.

"The men you killed today were brothers and are the very men who killed your king and queen ten years ago."

The bishop's eyes grew large.

"And they are the same ones who assassinated your queen today."

"That's where you are wrong," the bishop said. "The woman you killed today was not the queen."

Faruk was shocked by this news and appeared to be questioning himself, but he quickly recovered. "In any event, the person who ordered today's killing is the same one responsible for the assassinations of your king and queen so many years ago," Faruk said matter-of-factly.

The bishop straightened up and stared hard at him. With a tinge of respect, he said, "Tell me more, Royal Assassin."

They began to converse for several minutes.

Sir Michael looked on from a distance and saw what appeared to him to be two old soldiers having a casual dialogue. Bishop Kohlhaas finally stood and nodded his agreement. He called Sir Michael over and gave an order.

"I ask you to return with your men to the castle. Report to the court that all three men were caught and killed. Tell them my guards and I rode out to find Count Theo and Baron von Engel. I will apprise them of today's sad event and return as soon as circumstances allow. Say no more than that to anyone. Anyone!"

Sir Michael nodded in understanding.

The bishop continued. "The prisoner will come with us. If there are any further inquiries about him, say that he was silent before he died. Do you understand?"

"Yes, Eminence."

"Good," responded the bishop. "I can tell you that Saracen over there is an interesting fellow. But enough talk for now. I beg you to leave me your horse and return by foot to the castle for your report to the queen."

Without hesitation or further word, Sir Michael handed the reins of his horse to the bishop, gathered his guards, and departed.

The bishop told his men to tend to the Saracen's wounds and guard him closely. They had a hard and uncertain ride ahead.

10

THE KINGDOM FOREST AD 1130

Deep in the kingdom forest, Count Theo and Baron von Engel crawled to the edge of a ravine and looked down. Their eyes widened when they saw the size of the encampment below them.

"Do you recognize the banner?" asked Theo.

"It is Henry the Proud, Duke of Bavaria," replied the baron.

"Are you sure?" Theo pressed.

"Beyond doubt. I know it well."

They suddenly heard rustling behind them. They turned and saw they were surrounded by at least twenty soldiers. To make the situation more grim, the rest of their men were also captured and being led toward them by even more soldiers.

The knight commander of the group drew his sword and spoke. "I am Sir Harald. Stand and yield your weapons. You two, like your men, are now our prisoners."

Theo and the baron looked at each other. They silently stood and slowly drew their swords. They held them by the blades with the hilts toward their captors. Following a silent hand command by Sir

Harald, soldiers came forward, took the swords, and bound their new prisoners' arms behind them.

"What now, Sir Knight?" asked Theo.

Sir Harald responded. "Now? You will remain silent and do as you are told. We will take you to Henry the Proud."

The queen was in the throne room with Duke Teufelmund. He tried awkwardly to comfort her by patting her shoulder. Sir Michael entered the room. The queen looked at him eager for news. "What can you report?"

"Majesty, I have been advised to report that the assassins have all been killed. Bishop Kohlhaas met us on the edge of the forest and asked that I get word to you." Sir Michael briefly hesitated. "He took a small contingent with him to search for the count and the baron ... and to personally deliver the day's news. Highness, I am deeply sorry for the loss of Countess Marianne."

"Thank you, Sir Michael. This was an unexpected blow to us all," she said.

"Yes, quite ... unexpected," injected Duke Teufelmund. "And what of the assassins, Sir Michael? Did they speak before they died? Had they been sent by Henry the Proud?"

Sir Michael paused and then responded after finding the right words. "There were no speeches before those murderers met their fate. I am not aware with any certainty, Your Grace, how they came to the kingdom or who sent them. It was only clear that they were Saracens and the ones responsible for carrying out today's tragedy."

The queen turned to Duke Teufelmund. "Please check with Sir Ducu on the preparations of our armaments in the event we must mount a defense of the castle."

The duke bowed and wordlessly exited the throne room as the queen motioned Sir Michael to remain.

After observing the duke's departure, the queen looked to Sir Michael. "You have served our kingdom well for many years, Sir Michael. You have my trust, and I wish to freely speak with you in confidence."

"Absolutely, Your Highness."

"Sir Michael, do you not see a similarity between today's events and the murders of the king and queen some years ago?"

"There is no mistaking the parallel, my queen," responded Sir Michael. "Whoever was responsible for the death of your parents—"

"—is almost certainly responsible for the death of Lady Marianne," said the queen to complete the sentence.

"Majesty," replied Sir Michael. "This would almost certainly mean someone other than Henry the Proud."

"Precisely," noted the queen emphatically. "I ask that you keep this discussion strictly between us."

Sir Michael bowed in understanding.

"Please keep your eyes and ears open. And for now, I must prepare a funeral for my dearest friend."

Theo and the baron plodded along on horseback deep into the kingdom forest. They remained under heavy guard as they entered Henry the Proud's encampment. Their arms were still tied behind them, but their hands were free enough to hold the rear of their saddles for balance.

It was obvious to Theo that this ruler was more than simply Henry the Proud, Duke of Bavaria. He was more like a king or even an emperor. According to the baron, Henry owned vast territories in addition to Bavaria; these included Saxony and Spoleto. The camp and all its trappings were quite impressive and suggested significant wealth. As they continued to ride farther inside the massive bivouac area, the count and the baron exchanged knowing glances. They realized that the kingdom might be in great peril since they would be hard pressed to defeat such an army.

They were led to the command tent and were given help to dismount. Before he entered the tent, Sir Harald said, "Wait here." They did so and continued to drink in all the wealth and majesty before their eyes.

"What now?" asked Theo a few moments later as Sir Harald exited the tent and approached them.

"You two!" commanded Sir Harald to Theo and the baron. "Come with me and remain silent unless spoken to."

They nodded in understanding and entered the tent.

Before them was an impressive throne room, particularly for a field setting. Sitting in the center was the imposing figure of Henry the Proud. They briefly stopped but were pushed forward by Sir Harald. They walked slowly toward the throne until the knight put a hand on their shoulders to stop them. Theo and the baron bowed their heads.

"Why do you spy on me?" roared Henry the Proud in a deep voice that matched his appearance.

"Your Grace," responded Count Theo calmly but with firmness, "our kingdom heard of a large force in our forest being led by you. We were sent to confirm this and determine your intentions."

"And you expect me to believe this ... this story?" Henry roared.

Baron von Engel raised his head and said, "It is the truth ... cousin."

Henry the Proud turned his head slowly to the baron and stared incredulously. After a brief pause, he spoke in a more normal voice "Is that you, Wolfi?"

Theo mouthed the word *Wolfi* quizzically not believing what he had just heard.

"It is I, Henry," replied the baron.

Henry commanded, "I ask for privacy with our guests! Loosen their bonds and give me the room." He looked around the tent as Sir Harald and the others departed after freeing the count and baron from the ropes around their arms. "Now, my dear Baron Wolfgang Alexander von Engel, cousin, come forward with ... with ...?"

"Count Theo of Tyrol," stated the baron as he rubbed the circulation back into his arms.

Henry looked at Theo, studied him carefully, and motioned him to move closer. Henry continued speaking as he turned to the baron. "It is good to see you, cousin. It gives joy to my old, tired, and battle-weary eyes."

"And to me as well," responded the baron.

"Now," replied Henry the Proud, "before we drink and forget that chivalry forbids lies, what is this really all about?"

"The truth is as Count Theo spoke," said the baron. "We are here at the behest of our beloved Queen Margarethe to determine if our kingdom, my adopted kingdom, is threatened."

"Ask me whatever you wish either of you," Henry said. "As the baron can confirm, I do believe in our noble code of knighthood and will speak the truth."

Theo bowed in belief and asked, "Are you here, Sir, to invade our kingdom?"

"No," said Henry without hesitation. "We have just recently fought the Hohenstaufens and are simply passing through your territory on our way home to Bavaria. You have nothing to fear from me, son of Sir Josef."

"You know of my father?" asked a surprised Theo.

"He saved my life during the crusade," replied Henry. "And the lives of my cousin here and King Johann's. And many others as well. He was not then a knight but was actually a Non-Noble Templar."

"My father was a ... a Templar?" Theo was even more surprised.

"Yes he was, Theo," the baron said. "As am I!"

The baron reached under his neck armor and pulled out a chain with a Knights Templar symbol hanging from it.

"And I," stated Henry the Proud also producing a Templar symbol on a neck chain.

"And I," shouted Bishop Kohlhaas as he entered the tent with Sir Harald in tow and tugging at his arm. The bishop jerked his arm away from Sir Harald's grasp. Signaling his approval for the bishop to stay, Henry waved the knight out of the tent with a motion of his hand.

Bishop Kohlhaas pulled a chain from his neck with the Knights Templar emblem. "Despite time and distance, we Templars try our best to stay in touch with one another and keep ourselves informed."

Count Theo was momentarily overwhelmed, but he recovered himself. "Bishop Kohlhaas! I am glad you are here. But why have you come?"

"I am here bearing difficult news for all but especially for you, Theo."

"News?" asked Theo. "The queen? Who? What?"

"The queen is safe," the bishop said. "As are your and the queen's children. But I am deeply distressed to tell you Countess Marianne, your loving wife, is dead."

Theo winced and staggered. Though the baron was himself shocked, he helped steady Theo.

"But ... how?" Theo asked.

"By an assassin's arrow ... the very same scenario as with King Johann and Queen Annemarie," replied the bishop.

"But why?" cried Theo. "Who would do such a thing?"

"It has become clear to me that hired assassins mistook Countess Marianne for the queen as she strolled through the castle garden with your daughters, Lady Cristina and Lady Stephanie. And the man responsible for this terrible deed was behind the murder of the king and queen those many years ago. I have just learned who that man is."

Count Theo felt his body tense, his senses sharpen, and his mind focus on a singular goal to confront this villain and mete out justice.

Queen Margarethe sat on her throne pondering. Led by Anke, the royal nursemaid, the four girls slowly entered looking sad but holding hands. They walked straight to the queen, who embraced them. A moment later, Duke Teufelmund entered the room.

"Any word yet from Bishop Kohlhaas or Count Theo or anyone concerning the pending threat from Henry the Proud?" the duke inquired.

"No word yet," remarked the queen. "How goes preparations with our forces?"

"Preparations continue," the duke said. "But we must build up our stores of food and water in the event of a siege."

"Indeed. Please see to that," said the queen, "while I plan for whatever else is to come during these uncertain times."

Duke Teufelmund bowed and exited the throne room while the queen hugged the girls. She was deeply troubled by the future and many questions. She was worried not for herself but for these children and the kingdom. A single tear ran down her cheek, which she quickly wiped away so the girls would not see it and perhaps become more troubled than they already were.

Theo sat alone in a corner of the tent and was deep in thought as Bishop Kohlhaas, Baron von Engel, and Henry the Proud conferred near the throne. Theo looked up and noticed that the three men continuously nodded in agreement and indeed seemed to form a special brotherhood. They clasped arms in a circle as they stood and turned to Theo.

The bishop spoke first. "So Theo ... now you know the terrible truth surrounding the assassinations including the man responsible. I have shared my knowledge with you and my Templar brothers here. It is much to absorb especially when added to your personal suffering. You must now call on your honor, your training, and your chivalry as never before. But we wish you to do so knowing you are not alone in the quest you must undertake."

Count Theo slowly and deliberately looked at the bishop, the baron, and Henry the Proud.

Bishop Kohlhaas continued. "Theo, you will need strength for what lies ahead. We are here to offer it to you. Baron von Engel, with the consent of our gracious host, will explain more."

"Theo," the baron said, "there are three categories of Knights Templar: non-noble sergeants such as was your father, chaplains such as Bishop Kohlhaas, and noble knights as are my cousin Henry and I. We achieved this recognition during our final struggles and ultimate victory in the crusade. However, known only to the Templars was that your father, Sir Josef, was secretly elevated to Noble Knight Templar status. King Johann, who was also a Noble Knight Templar, conducted the private ceremony later the same day your father's knighthood was bestowed. Sir Josef is the only known person to have received multiple Templar designations."

Henry the Proud began to speak. "Theo, as both man and boy, you have fought the Saracens as have we here. All of us agree you have proven your worthiness, and if you accept, that you be added to the secret ranks of the Noble Knights Templar."

An inspired and grateful Count Theo again looked at the trinity of Templars before him. With deep determination, he responded, "I accept this great honor on behalf of all whom I love and serve—my God, my queen, my kingdom, my family, and my comrades in arms."

A brief ceremony was then quickly and quietly conducted that included a special blessing from Bishop Kohlhaas. Baron von Engel presented Count Theo the Knights Templar chain and pendant. As he hung it around his neck, he explained to Theo that it was the one that had been prepared for Sir Josef. At the request of King Johann, the baron had held it in anticipation of this moment.

Henry the Proud presented Theo with a Knights Templar surcoat with red cross, a helmet, and a full suit of armor. "I wore this in the crusade," uttered Henry with pride as he reminded himself of his youth.

"I shall be ever grateful to each of you for this great honor," said Theo. "We must return to the kingdom and confront Duke Teufelmund with the truth. It is now upon me to ensure swift and certain justice is meted out for his shameful and unforgivable misdeeds."

11

Innsbruck, Austria
Present Day

Otto observed that Carmen was totally absorbed in the story as was Cubby, who appeared to be almost beside himself.

"So Count Theo is going to challenge Duke Teufelmund?" she asked.

"Are you kidding?" injected Cubby. "You want to know what's coming? It's the Jedi Knights versus the Empire. It's Batman versus the Joker. It's the gunfight at the OK Corral!"

"The gunfight at the OK Corral?" asked a perplexed Otto.

"Part of our American western culture I'm afraid," said Carmen. "My brother likes old western movies. It's a story for another day."

Otto laughed quietly and nodded in understanding.

Cubby remained wound up. He made fists and started dancing like a prizefighter. "It's no longer Count Theo ... it's Count Terminator. And he ain't saying, 'I'll be back.'" Cubby gave his best Arnold Schwarzenegger imitation. "It's 'I'm coming back, sucka! And I'm going to show you what time it is!'"

"For Pete's sake, Cubby," said Carmen. "Enough already!"

"Come, come," exclaimed Otto. "I think you both understand that the end is drawing near. May I proceed and finish?"

"Absolutely ... but Carmen is hurting my self-esteem," noted Cubby with a feigned complaint while sticking out his lower lip.

Carmen gave Cubby a casual slap on the arm as she had a hundred times before. He gave her a look that could kill, turned to Otto, smiled, and winked. Cubby believed he had just won the latest bogus battle in the never-ending war between brother and sister.

Otto waited a moment until both were refocused on him and clearly anxious to continue. He had their riveted attention and began to share how the final events unfolded so many centuries earlier.

12

The Kingdom Castle AD 1130

As she heard guards begin to shout, Queen Margarethe handed the children off to Anke, their nursemaid. The queen ran to a window in the throne room and saw a great cloud of dust in the distance. That could mean only that a large force was moving toward the castle.

Alarms were sounded, and Duke Teufelmund entered the room trying to buckle his armor vest. "Help me with this nonsense!" he demanded, obviously upset with the evolving situation. The queen complied.

The duke continued fuming as she assisted him with his armor. He grew more nervous and sarcastic. "Something must be amiss with our advance party. No word yet from brave Count Theo, that baron of nothing, or your overbearing bishop?"

The queen backed away from him with a look of shock.

The duke persisted. "They ... they have *not* served us well!"

"Say no more!" shouted the queen in an effort to have him stop.

Suddenly, Sir Michael knocked, entered, and announced, "Majesty! You must come to the battlement and see for yourself."

"Yes, we must," the duke said sarcastically as the developing events began to irritate and overwhelm him even more.

The queen knew him all too well. He always acted like that if he felt he was losing control of a situation.

They exited the room as Sir Michael led them to the battlement. They looked down over the wall and saw a single figure at the head of a vast army. He was dressed in full armor as a Knight Templar and approached the castle drawbridge alone.

The queen noticed Bishop Kohlhaas and Baron von Engel off to the side. There was another imposing figure next to them she did not recognize. She scanned the area carefully but did not see Count Theo. She remained silent but suddenly began to sense with a slight smile that the kingdom may not after all have been in mortal danger.

The Knight Templar spoke in a bold, commanding voice. "I demand to see Duke Teufelmund!"

The queen immediately realized it was Count Theo speaking and put her hand to her heart. The duke, however, did not yet grasp with whom he was dealing.

"Who dares make demands of the royal consort?" the duke said loudly.

As he removed his helmet, Theo responded, "It is I, Count Theo."

"What mischief is this?" asked Duke Teufelmund as he turned to the queen. She said nothing; she continued to gaze at Theo, whom she thought looked magnificent and was as commanding a presence as she had ever seen.

"Lower the bridge," ordered the duke. He realized he had no other choice. "Approach!" he said to Theo.

The queen continued looking on as the bridge lowered. Theo rode slowly into the castle courtyard with the bishop, the baron, and Henry the Proud following a short distance behind. The loud clip-clop of the horses' hooves on the drawbridge echoed throughout the castle. Sir Harald also trailed the group as he held the reins of a horse carrying a hooded figure.

The queen stopped at the balcony overlooking the scene. She saw Duke Teufelmund walking hurriedly down through the castle as fast as his armor allowed. All the key players arrived inside the courtyard about the same time as the queen continued to observe from above.

"Do you wish to speak in public or in private?" inquired Duke Teufelmund as he approached Count Theo.

"I wish to speak in the garden," responded Theo as he dismounted.

Duke Teufelmund motioned Theo toward the garden. The pair moved slowly due to their armor. The queen closely watched the drama as it developed. She told a nearby guard that she would go to the garden area and that if any of the children should turn up, he should advise Anke to keep them safely away.

All parties continued to the castle garden, but during the short and silent walk, Duke Teufelmund felt his heart beating more rapidly. A growing realization started to grip him that his situation was serious and beyond reasonable control. He began to feel resigned to his fate, but that feeling of resignation was actually starting to give him strength. The duke stopped and faced Theo.

"Enough of this theater, Theo," snapped the duke. "What is all this madness? Speak your mind!"

Theo responded and all present in the garden area could hear him. "Duke Teufelmund, I publicly charge you with treason. You have sinned mortally, broken the code of chivalry, and plotted against our kingdom and its rulers."

"Nonsense!"

Theo continued. "Did you not hire assassins to kill King Johann and Queen Annemarie?"

The queen gasped audibly.

"Of course not," replied the duke. "Why would I?"

"To ultimately take control of the kingdom," answered Theo.

"But there ... there is the queen!" responded Duke Teufelmund as he pointed to Margarethe.

"No thanks to you," Theo said bitterly. "You tried to have her killed, but your fool assassins took the life of Countess Marianne, my wife, instead!"

The silence throughout the garden was palpable among the many who were present.

Queen Margarethe for the first time realized that the assassin's arrow was actually meant for her. Marianne had unknowingly given her life for her friend. The queen's jaw dropped and she grasped the railing overlooking the garden. Tears began streaming from her eyes as her head fell to her chest. Multiple realities simultaneously struck her very core.

"Lies!" she heard Duke Teufelmund shout. "All lies. Who claims these falsehoods?"

Theo simply responded, "The assassin you hired."

"I hired no assassin," claimed Teufelmund.

"Sir Harald, bring him," ordered Theo.

Sir Harald helped the bound and injured prisoner dismount. Faruk pulled back his hood and slowly limped forward. All eyes were upon him. He stared at the duke, lifted his bound hands, and pointed at the accused.

Duke Teufelmund looked stunned and shook his head. He looked around the garden. He saw nothing but disapproving faces including that of the shocked and incredulous queen.

Count Theo drew his sword. "Defend yourself, villain!"

Teufelmund turned this way and that. He saw he was trapped. Formed by bitter reality, a shadow crossed his face. But the queen noted a sudden strength and resignation in him as he looked up at her.

He faced Theo. "You may win the accusation, peasant boy," he seethed, "but not this fight!"

The expert swordsman drew his weapon and lunged at Theo, who despite the heavy armor, adroitly stepped aside. Teufelmund turned and the swordplay began in earnest. Both men carried heavy swords. Everyone understood that the fight may be epic but brief due to the sheer exhaustion of the combatants due to their heavy armor. All also knew with certainty that it would be a fight to the death. No quarter would be asked for or offered.

The queen watched from on high as the two men tried to move as well as they could with their heavy armor and the constraints of the garden. The duke drew first blood as Theo missed swinging left and, with his adrenaline pumping, the duke swung backhanded and struck Theo's body just below his right armpit. Theo felt his side and struck back with two quick swings that Teufelmund parried with a slight grin.

They took two steps back, paused, and rushed at each other. Their swords clanged. They turned and stepped in close to one another. With their free hand, they each grabbed the other's sword hand by the wrist and fought to a draw. Both began breathing heavily and struggled to push each other back.

Suddenly, Theo raised his sword hand higher as he lowered his left hand, which tightly grasped his opponent's wrist. When the duke briefly lost his balance, Theo bashed the duke's face by pushing the hilt of his opponent's sword into it.

The duke stumbled backward and began bleeding profusely from his mouth and nose. He spit out his front teeth. He regained his balance, smiled menacingly through his blood-covered face, and rushed Theo with a guttural yell.

Theo fooled his opponent by looking left but moving right. Teufelmund's heavy sword slashed downward but struck only air. The point of his sword went into the ground, forcing him clumsily into an awkward angle against the hilt of his sword. At the same moment, with the duke momentarily distracted, Theo spun and swung left. He caught Teufelmund's back with a deep cut through the chainmail below his shoulder. Exhausted, they staggered back to gain balance, and both were breathing hard and heavy.

The queen watched fearfully from the garden balcony as each man struggled to best the other. She instinctively started praying to St. Boniface to give Theo strength.

The others present were stoic and watched in silence. The only sounds were the men's heavy breathing and their multiple sword strikes.

Teufelmund turned and faced his opponent with a toothless grin and made a final rush. Theo stood upright while holding his sword with both hands as it pointed straight up in front of him. The duke attacked frontally. Theo parried, swung his blade parallel to the ground, and struck Teufelmund's waist even more severely than before. Teufelmund stopped in his tracks, dropped his sword, and twisted clumsily toward Theo. He fell to the ground mortally wounded.

Theo walked slowly to the duke, who began gasping blood as his upper body balanced on his right arm. "The kingdom will never be yours to rule," said Teufelmund.

"Nor yours it seems," replied Theo through heavy breaths. "But it will be for the queen and her children."

"Fie on the queen!" the duke said between coughs. "And her girl children."

Queen Margarethe was stunned as the fight reached its climax.

Theo stared at the duke and said, "For King Johann, Queen Annemarie, and Countess Marianne." With both hands on the hilt, Theo thrust his sword straight into the Duke's breast armor, through his black heart, and out the back of his armor until the ground stopped the blade. Teufelmund died instantly. The sword stood above his chest in the form of a cross. His arms fell lifeless on the grass.

Count Theo appeared physically drained. He fell to one knee as he grabbed his right side and saw the blood on his hand. His red-stained fingers quivered. He was overcome likely more with emotion than pain. The queen and the baron rushed to him.

The baron reached him first. They were initially silent, but the baron nodded approvingly with pride. The queen arrived next to them with great concern on her face.

Theo looked at her and said, "My queen. My sword and everything I have will always serve and protect you and the kingdom."

"Theo!" she responded as she touched his cheek gently with the back of her hand, "It has always been so, and so shall it continue forever. Our kingdom and I are deeply in your debt."

She then leaned in close, took his head in her hands, and whispered something in his ear. Theo's look of pain turned to puzzlement. But he suddenly realized what she had so privately revealed, and he smiled as he still breathed heavily. Nodding expectantly, he looked directly at Margarethe. She nodded with certainty and a smile to confirm what she had just shared only with him.

The queen stood. "Baron, please see to the count's wounds. I must now be a queen and welcome our guest from Bavaria. There is much for us to discuss and much healing to take place in the days ahead."

She placed a hand on the baron's shoulder. "I am thankful to so many, but please know I am especially grateful to you and all you have done for the count, for me, and for our kingdom."

The baron bowed, smiled slightly, and turned his attention to Theo as the queen majestically strode away in the direction of Henry the Proud.

After the queen had departed the garden with her welcome guest and most others, Bishop Kohlhaas walked up to Faruk and cut his bonds. "You have kept your word, Saracen, as will I. You are free to go. But I trust we will neither see nor hear from you again."

"Of that you can be sure," responded Faruk. "I am but a simple mercenary and do whatever I need to do for gold. I care nothing for politics or revenge." He paused. "But may I ask a question?" The bishop nodded. "Did you tell Count Theo I was the one who killed his father?"

"No," responded the bishop as he stroked his beard. "Let it go with us to our graves. That brave man already has enough wounds on his soul that need healing. I now see a clear path for joy and balance in his life ... and also that of Queen Margarethe."

Faruk nodded with understanding, looked at the castle before him, and sincerely announced, "May mercy, peace, and blessings be upon them." He turned to the bishop. "And upon you."

EPILOGUE

INNSBRUCK, AUSTRIA
PRESENT DAY

"So now you know the story of the kingdom queen. What was most significant to each of you?" asked Otto with great sincerity.

"The importance of chivalry," said Cubby.

"The power of love," responded Carmen.

"I think you are both correct," replied Otto with pleasure and a smile.

He saw Friederun, who suddenly arrived in the Silver Chapel with food and apologies.

"Sorry I took so long for lunch. I brought you all sandwiches. I hope I haven't kept you waiting too long."

All three shook their heads no and motioned with their hands that all was good.

"Great, then. All's well, children, and for a change, your father will be home early tonight. We should go, do some final shopping, and maybe wash up before dinner."

Cubby spoke up. "Mom … just a second please." He turned to Otto. "Can you briefly tell us what happened to the people in the story?"

"Well," replied Otto, "Henry the Proud and his army departed the kingdom and continued their journey home. Before leaving, he invited Baron von Engel to join him, but the baron decided to go to Portugal."

"Why Portugal?" asked Carmen.

"Because there was talk of a Second Crusade, and Portugal was the place where the initial vanguard of Knights Templar was forming. The baron saw his duty there since things seemed rather settled in the kingdom. In fact, he convinced Sir Harald, Henry's best knight, to join him. And you remember Faruk? He traveled to Spain, passed himself off as Saracen royalty, and married into a noble Moorish family," Otto said with a laugh.

"And what about Bishop Kohlhaas?" Cubby asked.

"Ah," noted Otto. "The good bishop continued to serve the kingdom for a few more years before he was called to Rome by Pope Innocent II. He was named a cardinal of the church. A short time later, in a secret ceremony, he became the chief chaplain and protector of the Knights Templar for the Vatican."

"Okay, okay," said Carmen looking first at Otto and then at her mother who obviously wanted to leave. "That's all great. But please, what of Queen Margarethe and Count Theo?" She held her hands to her chest while raising her eyebrows in hopeful anticipation.

Otto paused, smiled, and responded. "I think you will be very pleased to know that they married and lived ... well, happily ever after."

"And the girls?" asked Carmen. "I'm guessing all four girls were Count Theo's?"

"According to legend, that would be a good guess, Carmen. But you should know that they later had a fifth daughter ... Princess Jennifer. All five of the girls grew strong and healthy, and each became a queen in her own right. But those are stories for another day."

"Many thanks, Otto," said Friederun. "You have been most gracious, and I rarely have observed the children maintain interest like this. Especially if there isn't a smartphone or computer involved." She and Otto smiled. "And oh," said Friederun glancing into the chapel and pointing. "What's up with that kneeling knight there on the wall?"

Carmen grabbed her Mom's arm and began leading her to the stairway out of the Silver Chapel. "Cubby and I will tell you and Dad all about it at dinner."

They walked down together to the main entrance of the Hofkirche.

"Fare-thee-well, children," said Otto. "And oh, I almost forgot. I have a small souvenir for you both." He reached into his vest pocket and took out something with his hand closed. He opened his hand to Cubby. It was a coin with the Knights Templar cross. He then turned over the coin to reveal an infinity sign he showed to Carmen.

Otto handed the coin to Cubby, who flipped it to the Knights Templar side. “For you, Cubby, to remind you of chivalry and respect.” He pulled out another coin and handed it to Carmen with the infinity side showing. “And for you, Carmen, to remind you of love and kindness.” He put his hands on their shoulders. “As you go through life, always remember that these two symbols are simply different sides of the same coin.”

He patted Cubby’s shoulder as the young boy beamed at him. Otto patted Carmen’s shoulder too, and she reached up and kissed him on the cheek. Somewhat embarrassed, he touched his cheek and grinned with pleasure.

They smiled at one another and started to leave. Cubby very demonstrably stepped in front of his mother and sister to open the church door for them. He was trying hard to establish himself as a gentleman and eagerly wished to display the code of chivalry and respect in action. The women smiled at him, tilted their heads regally, and exited. With expectant eyes, Cubby looked back to Otto for confirmation of his gesture.

Otto smiled broadly and made a dramatic and courtly bow. As he bent over, a chain fell from his neck with the Knights Templar symbol hanging from it. It was the same one he had described as being worn by the heroes in his story. Cubby’s eyes grew as big as saucers. Otto put a finger to his lips for silence. He dropped the chain back into his shirt as he looked left and right to ensure no one else had seen what had just happened.

In a loud whisper, Otto said, “It’s a story—”

“—for another day” said a beaming Cubby, who stared at the coin in his hand and looked back one last time at a gently smiling Otto.

The young man breathed in and out with a big smile as he exited the church with a special secret and a timeless tale he would carry all the days of his life.

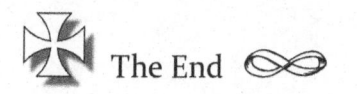

The End

AFTERWORD

Although a work of fiction, *The Kingdom Queen* was inspired in large measure by both history and multiple life experiences. These stretched from my childhood years growing up on Chicago's South Side to my great fortune to have lived and traveled throughout Europe for almost three decades. The story is loosely based on historical fact and personalities. It was initially triggered by a visit to the Silver Chapel area of the wondrous Hofkirche (Court Church) in Innsbruck, Austria.

The sight of a knight in armor kneeling at prayer high up on a chapel wall? Wow! It still prompts wonder. As a young man, I was thrilled with stories of knights and ladies fair in books, television, and movies. King Arthur and the many legends surrounding that Once and Future King were a particular favorite. The thrill remains.

The twenty-first century has been a difficult time for so many around the globe. We can all use some sunshine in our lives as well as a positive touchstone or two to guide us. My hope is that the kingdom queen may suggest and illustrate various themes—love, chivalry, loyalty, decency, kindness, and empathy—that, during our life travels, will help us achieve our best while, as circumstances allow, encouraging the same in others.

GLOSSARY OF CHARACTERS

Present-Day Austria:

Otto—Austrian tour guide and narrator of the story
Carmen—a thirteen-year-old American girl touring Europe with her parents
Cubby—Carmen's eleven-year-old brother
Friederun—Carmen and Cubby's mother

The Kingdom:

Margarethe—the princess who became the kingdom queen
Theo—a young man who overcame multiple challenges
Baron Wolfgang Alexander von Engel—Theo's mentor and surrogate father
Bishop Radbert Kohlhaas—head of the kingdom church and advisor to the throne
Duke Teufelmund—ward of King Johann
Lady Marianne—best friend of Margarethe
King Johann—ruler of the kingdom and father of Margarethe
Queen Annemarie—wife of King Johann and mother of Margarethe
Sir Josef—Theo's father and veteran of the crusade
Lady Lorraine—wife of Sir Josef and mother of Theo
Faruk the Assassin—leader of the Saracen marauders
Rami the Marksman—henchman of Faruk
Nijad the Tall—Rami's brother

Henry the Proud—Duke of Bavaria
Sir Ducu—the royal master-at-arms
Squire Michael—a kingdom messenger and later a kingdom knight
Sir Udo—captain of the guard
Sir Harald—knight commander for Henry the Proud
Squire Thomas—scout for Baron von Engel
Ingeborg—the royal cook
Anke—the royal nursemaid
Princess Victoria—daughter of Margarethe
Princess Allison—daughter of Margarethe
Lady Cristina—daughter of Marianne
Lady Stephanie—daughter of Marianne
Princess Jennifer—daughter of Margarethe

ABOUT THE AUTHOR

J. T. Page Jr. has a doctoral degree in business management from Nova Southeastern University. He served over twenty years as a U.S. Army officer, commanded military units on three continents, and is a decorated combat veteran.

He also worked as a Department of Defense contractor for almost two dozen years in Europe.

He has five daughters and nine grandchildren. He and his wife, Gretchen, live in Hawaii.

Printed in the United States
By Bookmasters